ISBN: 978-1-937543-88-4

All writings are works of fiction. Names, characters, businesses, places, events and incidents are either the products of the author's imagination or used in a fictitious manner. Any resemblance to actual persons, living or dead, or actual events is purely coincidental.

Published by Jaded Ibis Press, sustainable literature by digital means™ an imprint of Jaded Ibis Productions, LLC, Seattle, Washington USA.

Cover art and book design by Debra Di Blasi.

This book is in multiple formats. Visit our website for more information: jadedibisproductions.com

A Song of Ilan

a novel

Jacob Paul

Jaded Ibis Press
sustainable literature by digital means™
an imprint of Jaded Ibis Productions
SEATTLE • HONG KONG • BOSTON

for Francois Camoin
without whom this wouldn't have been this

a talmudical legend.

"Another anecdote of the Chief Rabbi Joseph relates to a question he often asked of orthodox members of his churches. He would in conversation say to a churchman:

"If you were on the bank of a river and your father and your rabbi were drowning, which one would you save first?"

Those who had not studied parts of the Talmud would say "My father."

Chief Rabbi Joseph would always say with a smile:

"You feel that it is your duty to your parent, but the Talmud says you should first save your rabbi."

—From the August 10, 1902, *The New York Times* obituary of the Chief Rabbi of New York, Rabbi Jacob Joseph.

Part One:

A Day

Standing on a small stone, Ilan flattens his palm against the cliff rising above the carriage road. Horizontal striations create roofs and ledges. From the smaller ledges, gnarled, bonsai cypresses sprout. Full trees rise out of the largest. Behind him, sitting on a low, stone wall that separates the carriage road from a steep wooded hillside stretching down to the Hudson River's plains, his wife rifles through her pack, a rustling that harmonizes with that of fallen leaves caught in the wind. Once there was a before, he thinks. A before in which this cliff was made of gray rock that, hewn to blocks, could build the Wailing Wall. Once there was a before; and the words are abstract. He tilts his head as if to examine the eighty-foot climb above. The words are sad in the abstract. The concrete events—a shooting in Tel Aviv; an escape to New York City; leaving the *derech*, the path of righteousness—are, well, concrete. Wailing Wall, he thinks. As at that famous relic, tufts of vegetation fracture the cliff's conglomerate rock. I have nostalgia for a period in which I had nostalgia, he mouths. The pain he feels is not for the passion with which he once prayed at the last standing wall of the old temple in Jerusalem, but for the young man walking whole Manhattan neighborhoods in a summer evening, awkward in his new secularism. It's for his wonder at junk stores on Mulberry spiked with memories of the Old City's Shuk, as if lower Manhattan's streets were equal exchange for stone alleyways two millennium old, a few stores selling knockoff watches and cheap baseball hats as colorful as a place where bins of fish heads divided crates of fresh eggs from street cobblers.

He looks over at the blue-helmeted woman who's begun scaling Horseman. She moves quickly, placing her hands and feet precisely in seams and on small protrusions. He tilts his head back further still to follow her ever-higher ascent and suddenly he loses his balance, steps backwards to stay standing. He wonders if he isn't maybe too... Too sick? Too sick to climb? No. Too something, what something? Scared? Too something, too drawn to the twenty-three-year-old wandering the windswept concrete fissures of lower Manhattan, chilly in his first real suit, desperate for the warmth of a bar, of a strange woman's smile. Too whatever, scared, yes, but off-balance really. Too off-balance to climb the "hard short thing next to Horseman" his wife mentioned over their omelets' darkening remains. Blue-helmet told him its name, Apoplexy. But knowing what to call the collection of minute ledges and tiny cracks that constitute a route up this section of the cliff doesn't make him feel much better about leaving the ground. He craves a cold or the flu, an emergency call from work or a car accident on the S-curves below, a sudden intervention and detention by Homeland Security.

Fuck it. Today is another day that Yedit has chosen to spend with him. If he can string enough of these together...If they can stay together through enough of these days there will again be a time in which Yedit is not, is not—he doesn't dare say it. There will be a time in which Ilan will feel comfortable even when he isn't wearing the black vest. There will be a time in which his wife's performance voice in city bookstores doesn't evoke a bullet wound in a young woman's chest, just inches above unexploded coils of nails and bolts and dynamite, an exo-viscera, a missed immolation.

There will be a time. Sure there will. But that time seems even more abstract than the words that sadden him. That time is like the cab ride home you've promised to yourself for right after you finish the drink you just ordered.

Blue-helmet moves effortlessly. Horseman is not a particularly difficult climb: a 5.5, first climbed just before America entered the Great War, by the man who till then held the record for reaching the highest point on K2. And that guy climbed Horseman in mountaineering boots with nothing but a hemp rope lashed around his waist, hammering homemade pitons into the rock for protection as he went. But Horseman is long, and it's exposed, and though Ilan's climbed it numerous times, his attitude towards it has been infected by his fear of Apoplexy.

There has always been fear. He and Louis, his first climbing partner, would travel to genuinely dangerous places. During slivers of sobriety they would scale ugly mountains in adverse conditions.

Blue-helmet, by contrast, neither conquers nor hides from fear. She just isn't afraid. Ilan no longer craves the fear but can't shake it either. Louis? Louis called a month ago to say that he was flying to Jackson Hole and driving to the Wind River Range. Early-season storms had finally made the k-cracks on Pingora worth climbing. Louis returned with tales of avalanches crossing the backpacking trail into the Cirque of the Towers, tales of packing an ice axe up five pitches of granite because the scramble above them had become a snow climb. Yedit, Ilan's wife and current climbing partner, isn't afraid either. Sometimes Louis' climbs appeal to her and sometimes they don't. But Ilan...Ilan can't tell the difference between ambitious and foolish because all climbs scare the shit out of him.

Yedit fidgets. Pieces of climbing gear, cams and hexes, clank and clash like a Nepalese pilgrimage, like men in red robes banging cymbals together to mark mountain progress. Gold sashes slung across their chests like the yellow webbing sling blue-helmet doesn't bother to take off of her own shoulder; blue-helmet doesn't hitch the tree that offers her first point of protection. Instead, she continues on to a stable stance at the base of a corner formed by the jutting cliff roof. Ilan knows Yedit wants him to stop watching blue-helmet. Gear up and get started on this Apoplexy thing. Blue helmets never stopped a war, Ilan thinks, but is he any more willing to fight? No. That's why he's here, not Tel Aviv. And is the color of this woman's climbing helmet in any way a remonstration for the elegant efficiency with which she places a cam in the rock, then clips the rope to its dangling carabiner in a motion that propels her further upwards still? The clanking and clashing softens to clinks and clacks, tricams and caribiners, just like that, his wife's almost ready.

And the breakfast nook, through whose sunroom walls Ilan and Yedit watched deer emerge from their property-line-woods and stalk the frost that marched across their lawn, uncut since the height of the Frisbee season, condemns him. And the thought of condemnation evokes a hint of overcoat, a hint of beach and asphalt, a hint of a hint he refuses to see. And that refusal, blended with the crick in his neck from watching blue-helmet's tensed brown calf protrude from green Prana capris, brings black spots into his vision. Despite himself, those spots puddle into images: his major in the Israeli Defense Forces standing on one side of him, a woman colonel on the other, facing a battery of news cameras; the cover of his wife's book jacket, on which the English, *Psalms,* in lavender, runs into the Hebrew, *Tehillim,* in burgundy coming from the right. Beneath the text a painting of Dovid with his knee in the small of Saul's back, Dovid holding Saul's head by his hair, a *shochet's* knife across his neck. In a fainter, more distant spot, Louis, Ilan's climbing mentor, passes a bottle of Armagnac to him as they cross an Alaskan glacier in the fog. But the spots quickly disappear, and for some reason, Ilan thinks of an old joke his father used to tell about a man who prays to Hashem that he might win 'a small lottery, a bisl gelt.' The rock ruptures the joke. An upset stomach turns Ilan's thoughts the color of a jet's exhaust, and he remembers the eager clapping and singing when the El Al jet landed at Ben Gurion, himself six months out of high school, just in time to do his time in the army.

Ilan walks backwards across the gravel carriage road that runs along the base of the climbs. He sequences the climb's moves, miming hand positions. It's useless. He's too self-conscious. The paint stains on his wife's sweatpants keep catching his attention. She's got a vagina under there, he thinks, and wants to touch—better to watch the blue-helmet climb, who from this angle is visible as she passes the collection of webbing and pitons that marks Horseman's midpoint.

Blue-helmet continues up the cliff, placing the occasional cam, clipping it to the rope on her left side, effortless. Still, Ilan inhales a little too quickly each time she swings for a hold or cuts out with her feet. Tell Yedit that you're not climbing then. You'll go home, make a pot of lavender Earl Gray. You'll sprawl on the pile of cushions and furs set in the living room bay window's recess. And Yedit, she'll put her head on your chest, your bodies a sickle, and read from the *Song of Songs*. In fact, you can read for the male speaker, she for the female. Except that Yedit's reimagining the piece with a single speaker who shifts gender and focus. So what. They'll read it in Hebrew. Forget the English. Make a fire. Except that he can think in Modern Hebrew but has to translate Biblical Hebrew into English. Think about climbing, asshole; and thinking about climbing rather than actually climbing is also a dodge.

"She chooses where she'll put gear before she gets there," Ilan says.

"She's probably memorized the climb."

"Perhaps."

"Are you climbing Apoplexy or should we keep walking?"

Ilan looks again. He can clip a pin about twenty feet up, and then about that high again there's a pocket where he might be able to stuff a pink tricam—a haphazard piece at best, hardly worth the time it would take to place. In other words, for the first twenty feet a fall means hitting the ground; then, after ten feet of relative security, the following ten feet also hold the possibility of a ground fall—if the pin's even any good. If not, one could consider the first forty feet absolutely unprotected. From there, another ten feet of challenging climbing brings one to a good cam placement and the second crux, a funky set of roofy moves, after which the climb is at least protectable. Blue-helmet's partner looks over at them and smiles. Her leader has led around the traverse and is now out of sight, around the corner and onto the face above the large ceiling formed by the striation.

"That's a really fun route," says blue-helmet's partner.

"I'd rather be warming up on Horseman."

His wife pays no attention to Ilan's banter with blue-helmet's partner. She's pulling on her harness. Ilan sighs; he once downloaded an Iranian porno in the repressed hope that the star would somehow remind him of the Palestinian suicide bomber he shot in Tel Aviv. Maybe, a small voice had suggested, the Iranian's body naked will let you imagine the Palestinian's body. Instead, he now confuses the porn star's body with Yedit's; he tries to imagine her breasts and recalls Persian nipples. He looks up at the climb, looks over at his wife; Yedit's harnessed-up and flaking the rope out of her pack into a neat pile at the base of the face. Blue-helmet's partner smiles over at him and he smiles back. Perhaps it would be easier with her. Maybe this woman would have let him fuck her in the morning before they came out to climb. And that's the thing about asking for miracles, if Hashem's willing to grant them, why does He need to create their occasion? If Ilan needs God to explain away the necessity of killing a woman, then he also needs God to not require the killing in the first place. Shit, he just needs God to tell him that Yedit will stay.

Ilan looks at his hands. His nails are scuffed and scratched. I have a weird resume he thinks. I grew up orthodox Jewish to Israeli parents in Pittsburgh. I returned to serve my military time in Israel. I spent a year in southern Lebanon working with Christian militias. While off-duty I prevented a suicide bombing at a Tel Aviv café by shooting the bomber, a Palestinian woman my age, twenty, twenty-two. I returned to New York to go to college but dropped out after a year. I became a financial advisor specializing in commodities and made a small fortune. I traveled with Louis to Alaska for a month and put up difficult routes in the coastal range. I met a hotshot academic five years my junior, married her, and bought a farmhouse two-centuries-old. My wife published a translation of *Psalms* that is a commercial success (bizarre as that sounds). I watched the World Trade Center collapse from my office window. It's quite the resume and yet what the hell does it say about me? No, Ilan decides, it isn't what I've done, or even what's happened to me. It's the dreams I've lost. And he wonders now whether the dream he's losing next isn't that of his lovely wife, Yedit.

You've begun to think in short dramatic soliloquies, Ilan notes. You're structuring your thoughts around these little phrases: 'a once in which there was a before,' 'there will be time,' 'fear,' 'miracles,' 'it's quite a resume,' 'the dreams he's lost.'

And from a distance, the tufts of vegetation look less like greenery and more like scribbled prayers wedged in the chinks between stone blocks.

Prayers, asshole? Ilan thinks. What would you pray for, hero-boy? That you weren't at the café? That the woman killed you?

That you could've fucked her before you shot her? That your wife didn't translate her translation? And a softer voice whispers, would your prayer just be *tihiyeh: you will be.* Ilan inhales and *My soul left when he spoke.* The Song of Song's fifth book. Except that his wife has translated it as: *soul left, exited, departed, went-out, in his words.* No, Ilan mutely yells at his wife, your heart left when you wrote. And yet he stays to read what she writes, doesn't he? Hope in her hopelessness? My prayer, he acknowledges, would be that I could pray. I'm weak and repulsive, he thinks. Disgusting.

Ilan's failure to take action towards climbing has so frustrated him that he thinks he might actually be motivated. Blue-helmet is long out of sight and has apparently stopped moving. He tries to divine his next move in the soft lines cornering his wife's mouth: *Elleh birechev v'elleh bisusim; and us, in the name of the Lord our God we will remember.* The comfort of chariots; the strength of horses. *V'anachnu kamnu*[1]. Sure, sure *we* rose up. Rose up and ran away. Killed and deserted. Shot dead your enemy and then left forever the country for which you killed.

"Diti, remember those kids in the park in Eureka?"

"Now he's nostalgic as well."

"Stop being so hostile."

"The kids with the dog with the eye."

"And the little girl thought it was a cattle disease but it wasn't."

"Ilan, really, are we going to climb today? Should we just walk down to Jackie? Would you rather lead that?"

Jackie is four grades easier, the same difficulty as Horseman. Yes, Ilan would much rather lead that. And no, he cannot bail on Apoplexy, though God only knows why.

"What was the name of that disease, Diti?"

Diti hands him the end of the rope; he's unprepared. "I don't remember. Here tie in."

"You don't remember?"

"What does it matter, Ilan? Tie in."

Last night, with Yedit safely asleep, to bed early in anticipation of climbing, Ilan pattered down to her office with his black Donna Karan vest and a roll of masking tape. It wasn't easy to find a night that he could make his own. Most usually she stayed up late wandering between her office, the bookcase lined foyer, and the refrigerator. Her office contained almost nothing. A laptop centered a six-foot wide white-Formica-topped table, itself in the center of the room, the kind of table that filled science labs when Ilan was in high school. A bookstand flanked either side of the laptop. One held *Shir haShirim*, the Hebrew edition of the *Song of Songs*; a Hebrew lexicology sat open in the other. A book light clipped to each bookstand. All the wires ran through a hole Ilan had drilled in the table to an outlet in the floor. Aside from the table and her desk chair, a leather design thing Ilan bought her on their first anniversary, the room was devoid of furniture and wires. The walls white, the floors the same ancient oak that's throughout the house. The uncurtained southeast-facing windows reflected black as he blinked in the overhead light. Careful not to disturb her bookstands, he spread open the vest on the table. He laid the first strip of masking tape, the stripe that holstered the explosive vials. Upstairs he heard rustling and froze. It subsided. A stair creaked and he froze again. The refrigerator clicked on. Ilan let out his breath and tore another strip of tape. A shorter piece that he laid across the first. *Is this why he can't climb? Because he was up all night? Because he's too tired?* He looked around Yedit's office. Two pictures hung on otherwise bare walls. One photo showed her birth parents: young eager soldiers dressed in green fatigues, standing, appropriately enough, in front of an olive grove on a kibbutz somewhere. The other photo was of the American couple that adopted her after her parents were killed: an oddly soft and dour pair seated on a pink couch. He'd drunk his morning coffee on that couch more than once. He went back to his tape and his vest. Delicate work. Every line must be precise.

"Can't we just go back to Eureka?"

"You seriously want to take a road trip through Nevada?"

He thinks, I am desperately searching her face for the hint of a smile. And then he thinks, 'desperately' and 'hint.' He thinks, I will never rise to her, to her occasion.

"Just let me analyze the climb a bit. Ok?"

Look at your wife, he commands himself, fumbling and fuming with his pack. Meet her eyes. She married him; clearly she's chosen to be with him. Oh, Yedit, he thinks, when you go from this life, will that unknowable intelligence of yours be forever closed? Your attacks simply cultured statements? Or do you expect to find yourself facing the giant scale that Chasidic folklore tells of, your good deeds stacked on one golden pan, your evil on the other. Do you do what you do in hopes of that final chance to turn away from that scale and finally confront the god you've offended beyond forgiveness? They say that one's *neshama* instantly understand the complete truth of God's plan at that moment. Will He simply send you back in a new form to try again? And if you are reincarnated, Yedit, will your parents again fall prey to a PLO shell fired out of Lebanon? A pesky small voice suggests that Ilan would love his wife more fighting an actual god than simply attacking a culture in a world bleakly undivine. Asshole, he answers this voice of himself. That woman will leave me long before she leaves this life, and when she does, she'll pack a few essentials, get into her Rav4 and leave no forwarding address. It was so much easier being twenty-three, showing off the negotiating skills he learned in the Shuk to Anne, to be stoked to date a blonde rich girl.

"Now or never, Ilan."

"I'll climb it. I'll climb it."

Pack finally off, he unbuckles the top-lid and loosens the drawstring securing the main compartment. Yedit touches the top of his head and he looks up at her. Bent over, he catches the line of her jaw, the silhouette of her nose blocking one apricot eye. She also would have shot the Palestinian woman, he thinks. Only she could have stayed in Tel Aviv.

Ilan extracts a purple Petzl harness, steps into its leg loops, and pulls it up until its waist belt sits over his hips, a few inches above the bottom hem of his sweater. He hauls on the straps on either side of the waist belt, tightening the harness, takes a deep breath, takes another deep breath, and tightens it some more. Of course, the danger is not of the harness coming off, but of the harness proving irrelevant because there are no cracks in the rock in which to place the gear that would catch the rope to catch the harness and in turn catch him. Nonetheless, he gives the straps an extra little yank. From above, a hollow voice yells, "Off belay." Blue-helmet's partner yells a thank you up rock, and unclips the ropes from her belay device. Freed, they dance up the cliff as blue-helmet pulls in slack.

Ilan begins transferring gear from the sling to his harness while blue-helmet's partner puts on her climbing shoes. Pulling the trigger on his purple Camelot, he watches the smooth action with which the four lobes, eighth-inch-wide metal half moons, two on either side of the trigger stem, pull back and then spring out. This is the joy of disassembling, oiling and reassembling a gun. Ilan no longer own a firearm, but spends hours on his couch, legs up on the coffee-table, flicking a Gerber knife open, observing its action, the work of the spring.

And then there's the precision of the masking tape bomb silhouette. After 9/11, his office temporarily shoehorned into the midtown branch, daily deliveries of baked goods began arriving from vendors, other branches, clients—some from the midtown employees. Then one day an angel-food cake showed up, frosted white with the city's skyline in blue, the twin towers done up as American flags. The masking tape boxes that run across the vest's black silk lining are meant to represent the parts of a homemade bomb—packets of drywalls anchors, vials of acetone peroxide, wiring—instead they remind him of a skyline, specifically, the skyline from the cake. He can't quite connect the two images, but he enjoys his mind's shuttling between them.

The two ropes tied to blue-helmet's partner's harness come taut, and she begins the—*on-belay? On belay. Climbing. Climb-on*—duet with her partner. "Excuse me, do you know if there are bolts at the top of Apoplexy?"

"I think so."

And she's off. In the time it's taken Ilan to mentally prepare himself, blue-helmet has scaled Horseman, built an anchor off the trees at its summit, and placed her partner on belay. Ilan loops a figure eight into the end of the rope that Yedit handed him. He could still make a last ditch run to the port-a-san. Tell his wife he has to shit again. Of course she would blame that on his having his first drink since they married last night. A glass of Louis' homemade wine. Louis brought the wine over to show off to Yedit. Ilan knew that, and so he drank a glass as well. Well, what promise was truly inviolate?

"Thanks. Could you wait until I put my shoes on?"

"Could you take any longer to do so?"

He didn't even taste the champagne that her editor brought over. That Saturday was nearly a year ago, when Joanne showed up at 9am with a bottle of Veuve Cliquot and a copy of the New York Times Book Review. It didn't matter what they wrote, she said, that an academic translation showed on their pages was "as rare as a lasting peace accord." Since that review, since his wife and Joanne's morning champagne drunk, a quick check for the burgundy row of her book's spines has become a mandatory stop at every bookstore within proximity. The project had defined their courtship—he got them into the botanical gardens and beneath the cherry trees she read him her *Psalms*, her wicked translations of *Tehillim*. Since, they've become her occasion for spending time with strangers, drinking with academics and reviewers and writers, drinking with successes. Since then, her contours, once dulled by intimacy, have sharpened. The way her skin curves across the top of her cheekbone. The way her dark lashes look as if she's permanently wearing eyeliner. The way she holds her head back and slightly to the right, in the same fashion as her mother in the office photo, so that her black hair falls to one side and her neck seems to rise towards unseen lips.

Ilan closes his eyes and forces himself to breathe. *Mercies of the Lord, forever I will sing of you*[2]. Ilan opens his eyes and forces himself to smile. He leans over and reaches into his bag for his shoes. Just when he thinks things can't get worse, the unmistakable sound of clanging hexes approaches, a mutant wind-chime, a breath of high altitude warfare. What could only be Louis himself stops a pace behind Ilan.

"Diti! *Mah nishmah*? You making this guy solo Apoplexy to set a top rope for you?"

"You can only lead a horse to water."

Ilan stands from tying his shoes, his spine's audible cracking smothered by Louis' loud laughter. And the blood rushing from his head makes him dizzy. As if there was ever any chance he would get out of leading this climb anyway. Louis plus Yedit is...well. When Ilan's mother slipped away from his father's deathbed to use the bathroom, Ilan's father leaned over and grabbed Ilan's sleeve. 'I'm afraid,' whispered. 'I'm too young.' Asshole, Ilan chides, nothing is that bad. Tonight he'll make lamb chops in a wine and honey sauce. Yedit will smile while she eats, her fingertips still raw from climbing. He'll tell her about the fear returning. She'll leave her plate and straddle his lap, hold his face in her cupped palms.

"How'd you like my Hebrew?" Louis asks.

"*Ivritekha beseder; aval mah karah lipanekha*?" asks Ilan.

"Whoa! Not that much Hebrew!"

Yedit scowls at Ilan.

"Right."

"I got nothing. *Beseder* maybe," says Louis.

"Just as well, buddy boy."

"You are still on belay, Ilan," says Yedit.

"And I still haven't tied my shoes."

"It's nine-minus. Fuck the shoes," says Louis.

"Nine-minus with no gear."

"If you can lead a 10a you can solo nine-minus."

"Fuck off?"

Yedit, rolling her eyes, scowling, threatens to translate what Ilan said about Louis' face if Ilan doesn't hurry up and climb. Louis demands to know what exactly was said about his face. Ilan hastily knots his shoelaces.

"You going to climb something, Louis, or just watch me?"

"Thought I'd keep your lovely partner here company, see how you flail, old chap."

"We're old fashioned, you can call my partner my wife."

"Did I tell you the one about the Muslim, the Jew, and the Hindu who go to a bar?"

"On belay?"

"For about ten minutes now."

"The Muslim pretends he isn't drinking; the Jew pretends he isn't paying; and..."

"Ok, climbing then."

"Climb on; please, I need to do work this afternoon."

"I've got another one. A Rabbi comes to meet with..."

"Enough, Louis, I'm trying to climb."

Louis grins. His lips are thin and his teeth seem to protrude directly from his dark skin. His eyes are black like Yedit's, and almond like Yedit's, ringed with eyeliner thick eyelashes like Yedit's. Next to each other, facing Ilan, their eyes could be siblings. Ilan wonders whether in Yedit's parents' day Israeli soldiers went to India to celebrate the end of their army service.

"Well get off the ground so I can entertain your wife. You like my jokes, right, Yedit?"

"Sure, Louis. You and your jokes, the whole package. Now if we could just finally get this climb underway so that I can get home and finish up Book Three."

Ilan pulls on a small shelf of rock inches over his head, tries to repress images of his wife surrounded by medieval rabbinic commentaries on the *Song of Songs* while he paces the house, shiftless and bored, and places the outside edge of his right shoe on a small lip of crystals protruding from the conglomerate rock, turning his right hip into the wall and stepping up. He places his left foot on another clump of crystals and slides his right hand into a two-inch thick horizontal crack at the outer limits of his reach. The stone cools his hand as it slips into the Palestinian woman's coat and he almost yanks it back out from the rock.

Breathe, he commands himself. Slow your heart rate.

And he breathes, but the blood pooling up through her clothes is both warm and cold on his hand. Pull open her coat, he whispers to the twenty-year-old with the gun. Pull open her coat so that you can see that she's a bomber that you had to shoot her. That you had to shoot her. That you had to shoot. Ilan grunts gutturally, loudly, and mantles up to reach high, forcing himself not to look into the crack as he passes it. Sure if she's a bomber then you had to shoot. And as he lifts his hand past his face on the way to a horizontal protrusion, moving his left foot onto a diagonal edge several feet up, he can't help but look for blood on his palms. Asshole, he shouts silently, and moves further.

He's off now. The ground is below, though not far below, several feet, five maybe. His heels are level with Yedit and Louis' conspiratorially close heads. Funny that they should be his life's two poles: the woman who eagerly slaughters God and the man who quite willingly fought religious rivals across a Kashmiri glacier. Deep breath and twist his ass right to weight his right arm; walk feet up into a layback; don't fall now; pull hard and jam a hand into a giant pocket in the rock, too wide for either scribbled prayers or climbing gear; keep weight low to make the open hand grip stick to the sloping rock; walk feet up with arms straight; stand fast and grab the tiny ledge with the right hand; another move and that's the pin; relax the calves. God damn it, Yedit, pay attention—stop talking to Louis. Get a draw off the harness; fuck, finger stuck in the carabiner gate; shake it loose, shake it loose; ok; draw in hand; left hand is getting tired; the woman crumples, she doesn't even crumple: she's walking then she's on the ground, no transition; keep it together; breathe; breathe; breathe out slowly while sighting down the barrel and gradually squeezing; breathe and shut the fuck up; clip the pin; good; reach for the rope dangling from the harness; fuck, slack, slack, slack; don't fall; pay attention to me; fuck; clip the rope; squeeze softly, squeeze slowly, squeeze at a point two inches left and three inches up from the sternum; rope's clipped; good; breathe. Ok.

Ilan shakes out his right arm, matches to the same hold his left hand was on, shakes out his left arm, and blinks his eyes and his mind. Clear your head, asshole. But it's as if his head is a Yatzee cup and every attempt to shake an idea free forms a new combination of disturbing letters. He remembers his parents picking a child's bicycle out of a mound of junk at a Jersey-shore thrift shop on a summer vacation. When he was afraid to try riding it in the store, they brought him a tricycle. For years afterwards, they cited his one-time fear to continue buying him larger tricycles, until he worried that eventually they would buy him one of the adult ones with an ice-cream vendor's box between the handlebars. And what good is climbing if the necessary focus the movement demands can't cleanse his mind? But there she is again, sauntering diagonally across the broad sidewalk towards his café table, now in a heavy overcoat, now in the Iranian porn star's white lace lingerie, now wearing nothing but lace-up stacked heel boots, a burqa flipped back to reveal her coy, down-turned grin, her legs crossed in a runway model's stride, the bullet wound just above her sternum. Why is she back anyway? Ilan wants to recite the *Shema*, but refuses to. The *Shema* is an old prayer, one of the few that's not meant as a replacement for one of the daily animal sacrifices made in the Temple. One should recite it three times a day, ideally. It's funny in that one recites it, much like the psalms, to ask God's help from danger. And one recites it at the moment that death is inevitable. All the famous martyrs tortured to death by the various occupiers of Biblical Israel died shouting the prayer's first line. He sees spots again, feels sweat forming between his fingers and the rock. It's been months, and before that, months too, since he even really thought about shooting the would-be-martyr. Ilan needs to regain some upward momentum. If you could just wear your vest. If you could just tattoo the aching ring above your sternum. Then goddamn Yedit's psalms. She doesn't believe, but he would. He would *daven* even. No, he cannot recite it, cannot possibly declare, "Hear oh Israel the Lord our God the Lord is One." He can have Yedit or he can have God, not both.

He begins climbing above the pin. It would be so wonderful to just lower off from here, let Louis finish the climb. But there's really no guarantee that the pin will bear weight anyway. Safer to keep moving. (Though if the pin won't hold his static weight, how's it supposed to hold the dynamic force of a fall?)

A series of sloping holds lies in front of him and he tries not to equate cold rock with cold barrels. He keeps his body weight low and places his feet carefully, moving further and further above the manky pin. A steel stake rotting out of the body it scars. He tries to concentrate on his breathing, slowly inhaling deep gasps of crisp autumn air. The temple was built without iron, without any metal that could be used for war. Ilan wants to know: is it that he's going to die here, on this climb, that she steps onto her heels so deliberately, practically goose-stepping. No, she shuffles. She shuffled towards the café, uncertain, hemmed in by pedestrians. She could have blown herself up where she stood, raised her arms and ascended. But those last few minutes alive, the time it took to walk all the way to the café, were too precious for her to sacrifice. And if those last few moments were worth living, filled with whatever one is filled with (*Psalms*), she can't have been at peace (*Shema Yisraeil*); he could have talked her out of it!

No, the street was clear, he sat sipping a double espresso garnished with candied orange peel and staring across the boulevard at a scimitar of beach between concrete high-rises and she strode toward him. The blue skies and rotting leaves enter his lungs. A musky campsite. His blood flow slows. And then he is thirty feet above the ground, at the secret pocket that just barely accepts a pink tricam. His forearms ache. He tries to visualize himself moving past this spot and instead pictures his fingers giving out. Why the fuck didn't he sleep last night? You don't want to know, the small voice whispers. His shifting feet take him towards her, his gun pointed at the bundle of black rags oozing oil on the ground.

Focus. He unclips the carabiner with all three tricams on it from his waist and lifts it to his mouth. If he could just con his left forearm into a relaxing a bit...He bites down on the pink one's strap; for every step he takes forward, the screaming ring of people retreat several; he lets go of the carabiner and reaches for the strap with his hand. He takes his left hand from the gun's stock and extends his fingers towards the stone lip that has become her coat's hem. And then his right foot and his body jerk downwards and he screams, "Fall!"

But his left hand holds on to the edge of her coat, clings to the rock, catches him. He brings his right hand up to the pocket where the tricam should have gone, would have gone if he hadn't dropped it; he replaces his feet on either side of her legs and attempts to regain his breath. But the tricams are gone; the tricams are gone and there is no other protection. And given the way Louis has scurried back from the climb, the tricams came very close to hitting him. Good, yet the Lord *Wrathfully-repelled the decimation of his servant's sword*[3]. Ilan inhales, and his breath brings in the heady scents of soy sauce and blood. Dead woman smell. Please, God, please, can't you let your faithful servant have even a little reprieve? Clinging to her coat, to her body, and shaking against the rock, Ilan promises that if he lives through this, he'll give a dollar to *tzedakah*. Not that he believes, of course, but he wonders, would that work? Would pledging the ceremonial dollar to charity, the act of *tzedakah* travelers promise to perform at their destination, transforming their trip into a mission to do a good deed, and thus summoning God's protective umbrage, work for a rock climb? He obviously can't give the money at the top of the climb. But now that he's already on the climb, he has to get down to give it. This is no time for brain-teasers. Besides, what is he? Some penitent clutching the edges of his *tallis* and beseeching Hashem? Ilan is no faithful servant. He's a sinner, a sinner! The small voice reasons, he meant it about the dollar—to the first person who asks, no judgment. He wishes he could let go of the Palestinian woman's body and willfully follow his tricams' arc to the ground at his wife's feet. But he cannot let go. Neither strong enough to kill, nor strong enough to die.

There is no gear for the secret pocket. Seven feet more and he can place a decent cam, gear that will actually hold a fall in all likelihood. But in those seven feet he will have to open the woman's coat. He will have to risk her exploding after all. He will have to risk her still being alive. He will have to risk her not having a bomb. *V'lo hakamoto be'milchamah*[4]. No, God did not prop him up, make him stand, or give him courage, in war. Ilan tries to breathe. If he falls now, he will hit the ground. Rather, he will hit the ground from thirty feet up in the air. He tries to think how many people who've jumped off fourth floor balconies live. Asshole, he reminds himself, that's an idiot thought. Think about Yedit.

Louis yells up to keep fucking moving. Yedit shouts to climb, keep climbing. Ilan lowers his left arm, shakes it out, puts it back up and shakes out his right arm. In the psalm, the speaker says that God has turned away by blunting the speaker's sword. But Ilan wonders if that's such a bad thing. After all, a body, a woman, a Palestinian woman, whom he shot, shot with his M16, lies between him and the cam placement. And what would have happened if hadn't shot her? the small voice asks. She would have blown up the whole café, Ilan whispers to himself.

"I'm thinking," Ilan yells down.

"This isn't the time, Ilan," Louis yells back.

"I see her crumpling."

"Nothing's crumpling, buddy."

"I can't."

"Get moving, buddy."

Below, he can see Yedit's teeth clamped down over her lower lip. She's too tense to speak, he figures, and yells, "I keep thinking about the *Song of Songs*, about the man knocking on his lover's door when she's inside with the other women."

"Not now, habibi," Yedit says. "I need to focus on belaying, you need to focus on climbing."

"But when she answered the door he was gone, her soul was gone, the watch guards of the city beat her when she searched for him in the streets," Ilan persists.

"You can't stop there, habibi," says Louis.

Or maybe she, the bomber, would have changed her mind. And then the great empty question of anti-terrorism presents itself for the umpteenth time: if the terrorist act responds to a mistaken and morally problematic act by the state acted upon, does that state then have the right to act ruthlessly to prevent that act? To which the question: How can anyone not act to save children from being torn apart by the old screws and rusty wire packed into a homemade explosive belt worn by a suicidal? The Palestinian woman was a girl, hardly religious to judge by appearances. An irrelevant side note, that. As if anyone believes it's the promise of virgins that drives men (and women) to martyrdom. You would do it if it meant absolution, the small voice whispers. You'll give the dollar. Ok, Ilan answers, but I can't say the *Shema*.

"Don't make me have to marry Yedit," Louis yells. "Don't die up there."

Sweat pours down his face and chest. If he falls he won't die 'up there.' He'll die on the ground right where they're standing. Sweat accumulates between his fingers and the rock. His own body lubricates his demise. His legs tremble. He'll fall. He is so obviously going to fall, so obviously wants to fall, and he can never love anyone after Yedit again anyway. I could have stayed drunk, he whispers to the rock. Hope is worse than hopelessness. I could have died feeling the way I feel. Why didn't you let me, Yedit, why trick me into this attempt at happiness? If he doesn't move he will fall, and if he falls, he will probably die. I don't want to be alone up here with a dead Palestinian woman, he whispers to the rock. And the rock plays back the Iranian porn star's thick bush and violet labia.

"Climb, Ilan; climb, please, please, please, habibi."

His arms ache. The coat's hem is thickening with blood, threatening his grip. The rock radiates cold that chills his sweat-soaked organs. His legs tremble (sewing machine legs, Elvis legs). He tries to lower his heels to take some pressure off his calves but the falling tricams keep dropping and dropping and dropping. He looks down; Yedit faces away from him. She's preparing to run backwards to take in slack. If he falls, she'll run in a desperate attempt to keep him off the ground. Always running to keep him from crashing. Finally, he understands why that second line of the *Shema* is meant to be whispered. Out of mercy. The martyr is dying, he's spent his last breath shouting: *Shema Yisraeil Adonai Eloheinu Adonai Echad.* He has no strength left. At best, if he lives that long, he can confess the second line to himself. Why make him feel that there was something more he could do? Better to require that he whisper it to himself, make mandatory the inevitable, that private reassurance at the very end.

"Come on, buddy; it's easy moves from where you are. Get to the roof."

Baruch sheim kivod malkhuto l'olam va'ed: Blessed is the name of his courageous kingdom forever and always.

"Ilan, you have to move."

He lifts his left foot, places it on an edge and pushes. He forces air in and out of his lungs, and then he moves his right hand, grips a rounded gray knob over his head and feels it dig into his fingertips. It bends beneath his pressure, he thinks; he thinks, I'm holding onto the cartilage in her nose. It can't possibly hold his whole body weight. He turns his head down and scrunches his face against the image of his hand pulling her cheeks from her eye sockets, against the image of his mother pulling chicken apart, and wills his elbow to straighten, his shoulder to relax, his body to hang from the hold. He seizes on an image of his house: a square stone farmhouse with a four-sided peaked wooden roof. It sits on a rise in the close-hemmed deciduous woods. This morning, they woke to strong sunlight through the east-facing bedroom windows. After pattering down the worn-wood stairs, Ilan observed frost in the crevices of the Adirondack chairs on the flagstone patio beyond the sunroom's glassed-in walls. The house is built out of fleece blankets, fabric softener and fresh-scented dishwasher-detergent. Ilan wants to curl on the living room couch with a latte and a magazine. What have you done to deserve such comfort? he wonders. If he falls, Yedit will run backwards, but that won't save him. He must climb higher, further away from her diminishing form. And in the disconnected glow of under-cabinet kitchen-lighting, Yedit shuttles away from him, or he shuttles away from her, Ilan can't tell which but that the house-image gradually collapses, his arms tremble, the Palestinian woman's nose twitches in his grasp. Moving upwards only increases the distance of the fall. Fuck you, asshole, he corrects himself, the length of the fall no longer matters: it's all too far. Another hand up, another move. If the space between not falling and safety is the length of the woman's body, then he's parallel with her breasts.

Yedit now pays attention to him exclusively. He can see, in his periphery, the cocoon from within which she isolates Louis, who continues to hang on her borders, whispering words she does not hear. Louis whispers that he and Ilan have climbed far worse. He whispers that Ilan once froze in the middle of an ice route in the Catskills after his feet blew out. Ilan hung there by his axes, his arms slowly giving up, dangling like a leaf melting out of an icicle. But then, as if by magic, Ilan kicked one crampon-tipped foot into the ice, and then the other, slowly began to climb again. Louis whispers that a god haunts Ilan, a deity who will neither disappear into ether nor offer salvation; Ilan wishes he could cast Louis' voice out of his head. Louis putting math to God, making God into an arithmetic, an algorithmic truth, a half understood minute dimension, a body of constants for equations of the unknowable.

Ilan wishes he could recapture the empty-headed climbing space he'd been in before the tricam incident. Ilan wishes that he wasn't lying to himself when he imagines a point in this climb in which he was one with the rock. Just make the moves. He ungracefully brings a thigh over her thigh, braces it against the rock, turns a heel into her side, pushes. His elbows stay bent and protruding, his knees splayed. Turn a hip in. Straighten your arms. Climb efficiently. But her body is in the way, pushes him out from the wall. He remembers Louis instructing him, back at the beginning, that if you couldn't do a move properly, you certainly couldn't do it by flailing. But Ilan cannot climb efficiently.

Say it, say the *Shema*. When did he last? On a plane flight? An amusement park ride? A roller coaster? To declare God would be to curse Yedit. He can't. He just can't. If he sides with God, believes in God, then he has to declare his wife, the woman he loves, the woman who's given him hope, a house, a life beyond drunkenness, he has to declare that woman an *apikoris*, a heretic, an enemy of God, unfit to live.

Then he's stuffing a number one Camelot deep in the crack beneath the roof. He's got the rope clipped into it. He's safe; he's past the lump of woman's body, looks down, sees nothing but rock. Another challenging twenty feet remain above him. The harder climbing. But it's safe. The cam makes it safe to fall.

He's tired. He reaches back to his harness and grabs another cam. The crack's big and forgiving, without much effort, Ilan finds a second placement. Using another sling, he equalizes the two pieces so that they share his weight, the force of his body. He calls down for Yedit to take.

"You're not coming down, are you?"

"What?"

"Don't leave all that gear up there, Ilan. You're safe."

"I just want to rest for a minute; can you take and hold me?"

Yedit pulls slack in through her belay device, her arms in front of her. He can feel the rope hauled taut against his harness. She jumps up in the air while pulling in more rope still, and then sits back in her harness, tugging Ilan upwards against his gear. He sighs. She jumped to take the extra stretch out of the rope without him asking. He loves her. Of course, that might also reflect her peculiar dedication to efficiency. Or, it might reflect a desire to show Louis that she knows the proper procedure. Or a reluctance to dispirit him so completely that he leaves a hundred bucks worth of cams in the rock. He lets go of the wall and leans back into the belay, lets the harness hold him. His breath comes easier and he pushes against the rock with his feet, dips his hand into his chalk bag, powdering up against his palms' unruly sweat; he smiles. See, Ilan tells himself, the cams hold; his gear works; nothing bad will happen. Men in light-blue protective suits slowly uncoiled the rows of explosives from the woman's body; marks of their fingers, their hands, cast in her coagulating blood. Bomb removed, her body lay there, discarded. Ilan stood guard, his rifle by his side. A body, he had thought, a human body. Either then or now, he can't discern which, his standing watch over the dead woman reminded him of his occasional job in high-school. The Jewish mortuary would call if a body had to remain overnight and none of the deceased's relatives were available. They would pay Ilan fifty bucks to stay in the lobby, reciting *Tehillim*. So the enemies of the Jews shouldn't desecrate our dead, he whispers to the rock and pushes with his legs, swinging out, far above Yedit's head, for our bodies are loaned from Hashem (The Name, God, The Name in place of the name of God), and our corpses must be returned to him. In the mortuary's gold-upholstered waiting room, the night was so silent that he wondered whether he read the psalms to help the departed *neshama* reach heaven, or to ask God to guard his own safety.

Well, he's safe now. If he falls at any point from here on out, undoubtedly, this same gear will hold his body weight. Yedit will catch his fall. Truly, he's safe. There's not much left to do. He quickly represses a question of how he will explain to his children (if he ever has them), if there is no Israel anymore.

The truth of the matter is that he wasn't alone at the café. Or not so much that he wasn't alone as that he sat at the outdoor table and watched the street because he expected Dalia and her father. He'd met them at the Sephardic synagogue he'd begun attending a year earlier. Or rather, he decided that he would keep attending that synagogue after Dalia's father invited him home after Saturday morning services for Shabbat lunch. They were Moroccan, had lived in Fez until expulsion in 1948. Their floors were covered in layers of Bedouin rugs, hammered copper lanterns hung over their dinner table, thick drapes made a permanent twilight of their apartment. Then Dalia and her mother brought out pickled fish with carrots, bowls of oil-cured olives, couscous with chicken and dates. Ilan waited for them at the café because the army would release him to civilian life in a month, and he would stay, a person returned to the land of his birth, the land of his people. He would stay, and he would marry Dalia, and they would live in The Land of Palestine, the land of their forefathers, the land of their birth, the land promised them by Hashem, *Eretz Yisroel.* Ilan waited at the café, and in retrospect, it was as if he waited before the creation of the universe, the formation of the *tevel.*

Ilan calls down to Yedit that he's climbing again. She pays out rope as he moves onto the first roof, working his feet up until his body is horizontal, his head pointing east past the Hudson. He tenses his abdomen while twisting his right knee over his left leg to reach high with his right hand onto the wall over the roof.

He wasn't alone, but he was also alone. Dalia and her father never made it through the security blockades. He wasn't alone, but he would be afterwards.

And he must have know Dalia was lost, that he was lost to wanting Dalia, because after the news conference, he agreed to a glass of orange vodka with the orange-haired woman colonel. By his second glass he agreed to take her up to the room the Israeli Defense Forces lent him. And so the orange-haired colonel, the press rep, was the first woman Ilan ever slept with. Afterwards, the Eli's store-sign cast noir through the Venetian blinds, and Ilan traced shadowed stripes across her breasts, raising soft goose bumps row by row, and she didn't stop him as he approached her aureoles. She was very young to have made colonel. Twenty-nine or thirty, most of a decade older than Ilan. He said that they'd had sex in a tone of quiet surprise, and she rolled her body towards him, her flexed abdomen accentuating the indentation between her inner thigh muscle and the stubble of orange hair, black in the dark light, pointing down. In the same tone, he said, "I killed a woman."

The colonel stood from the bed, pulled on her slacks, jammed her panties in her pocket, turned away to fasten her bra. Afterwards and alone. Ilan twists his body the other way and brings his left hand up higher still, admiring the line of muscle that tenses along his side from hip to shoulder. Inhaling deeply, he lets go with his feet and swings them over empty space to the roof's lip, and then he's reminding himself again to take the extra second to aim properly before firing. The Palestinian woman sort of sits backwards as she falls, then crumples. Sweating, Ilan stands up on the ledge, pops a nut into a waist-level crack, and forces himself to proceed. The sooner up this thing, the sooner off of it.

He will never move past Yedit. *I asked after her and found nothing*[5], reads the *Song of Songs*. Nothing, whispers the small voice. Why can't this new project, Yedit's translation of the *Song of Songs* be their second courtship? One more roof to climb over and he can come back down. For starters, it can't because she insists on mutating the text so that instead of two speakers of opposite genders addressing each other, there is only one speaker who switches gender. That's it isn't it, he thinks, she's re-reading it to be self-sufficient, to exclude me. She's translating a poem with two lovers into a narcissistic triumph of one loved poet.

Twisting his left hip in, he reaches his left hand upwards and leftwards to a ledge, matches feet, twists his right hip in, and brings his right hand onto the same ledge, finally letting go with his feet. *Bikashetihu v'lo mitzatihu.* His feet swing out into space. *I cried to him and nothing answered me*[6]. He stands up and walks towards the shot woman, black on the sidewalk between speckles and dabs of tar.

He approached her with his gun trained on her head, the sun above the beach catching his eyes as he left the shade of the café's awning. His legs crossed one another as he side-stepped towards her. Please, he whispered, please, God, let her be a bomber. He imagined her children when they realized their innocent mother had been mistaken for a martyr and shot. When he was within two steps, blood at once pooled past her body, running in lines down the cracks in the pavement. He gasped and jumped back as the liquid reached for his boots, and the crowd gasped and pushed back with him.

Ilan looks down at the space below. Yedit calmly feeds him rope, relaxed. *I called to him, and he did not answer; or, I cried to him, and there was no answer...I rose, I, to open to my dodi; I opened, I, and there was no answer; I cry to you, and nothing answers me.*[7] I cry to my wife, and nothing is all that whispers to me. Nothing is my lover; my *dodi* is nowhere. So why shouldn't Ilan have God at least? Louis gives him a thumbs-up and whispers something into Yedit's ear. But I am in this marriage, Ilan reminds himself. And you shot that woman, says the voice. Ilan's feet still swing below him.

He wonders that his thoughts move so quickly, the images so rapidly; his feet have barely been freed. He reaches down to the woman's coat, his legs on either side of her, the blood lapping at his boot soles, and, careful to not move her arms, grabs her collar. Ilan curses his mind and swings to pull his feet up, finds surfaces to push against, and mantles his way onto the ledge. He places another cam, this one to protect Yedit from a pendulum swing should she slip coming over this second roof. It'll be over soon, yes, soon the climb will be over, soon he will open the suicidal's coat, find the belt packed with nails and wingnuts and scrap rebar, lined with homemade, 'Mother of Satan' explosive. Ilan traverses over easy terrain to his right, and places a final, final cam.

He opened the woman's coat, carefully, slowly, listening for anything that might imply a trigger or a heartbeat. A sliver of breast showed along the edge of her shirt collar, brown flesh above a lace bra. If she hadn't been a bomber; if he hadn't shot her; (would she have fucked him), Ilan thinks. The explosive belt was plain to see. He touched the bit of exposed skin and felt tears in his sinuses. Don't cry, he ordered himself, panicked: don't cry! But the words, 'she's a bomber,' tasted of snot and mucus. Can I be sorry I've killed her?

Ilan asked himself. He threw her coat flap back down. Fast boot-steps closed in from behind. If he had asked her to sit down for a coffee with him when she reached the café; if they had talked about her linguistics classes at the university, about writing and war and books. He imagines her thick brown nipples tangled in his chest hair, her heaves beneath his body.

Ilan inhales deeply and exhales as slowly as he can. Once, while the house was being renovated, their joint possessions crammed into Ilan's Lexington Avenue apartment, Ilan took an afternoon from work to check out progress. All the laborers were gone while they waited for a coat of polyurethane to cure on the oak. Summer sunlight reflected from the trees in front of the house and cast green shadows on the living room floor's fresh polish. The city had been muggy, but here the air was soft. He phoned Yedit and told her to leave her office, get out of Poughkeepsie and come meet him. She unbuttoned her short-sleeve blouse in the driveway, left it and her denim skirt on the doormat.

"They said, no shoes on the floor while it cures," he'd said, and lifted her by her upper thighs, her sandaled feet wrapping around his waist, and carried her into the kitchen. The curing concrete countertops seemed dry. He set her on the seemingly dry countertop next to the stove, and afterwards there was the slightest of depressions, the contour of compressed ass pressed into the concrete's surface. The contractor polished the counters, grinding out the uplift, the cast of her ass, diamond grit turning cement down to dust, to crush. Ilan still runs his fingers over the spot while he waits for his morning coffee to brew.

A last, easy move brings him level with the thick trunk of a cypress tree growing out of a wide ledge. He wraps an arm around it, his fingers tracing grooves cut into the trunk by old slings used to build rappel anchors before bolts were placed on the wall behind the ledge. Ilan pulls himself up, climbing the tree as much as the cliff, and stands up on the ledge.

He's done.

The bolts are in front of him.

The Palestinian woman has been dead for a decade now.

Yedit's body is still a wonder to him. Her flesh, her corporeal being: the dwelling of her unknowable intelligence. Just this morning, after breakfast, he chased her naked fleeing form up their farmhouse stairs, catching the bedroom door moments before she could latch it, cornered her balled body against the wall, the middle knuckle of his left hand both bearing his weight and brushing between her labia. Her body contracted like a starfish as he anointed her forehead with a light kiss. He can't predict her, would never have anticipated that after releasing her, she would pin him against the mattress wall of their too-high bed, encircle his cock with her thumb and forefinger, and, crouching, close her lips around the base of his penis, pull away, come back, and then pull away again before releasing him, glistening, twitching, out of breath.

He slaps the tree. Its branches spread out at eye level, furry green fronds between which the Hudson valley unfolds like a colored desert floor seen from a Jerusalem mountaintop. He is safe. And who would have thought there would be these beautiful, stunted cypress here in New York State. He reaches out to the bolts, quickly clips a quickdraw into each, aligning them so that their carabiner gates open in opposite directions, clips the rope through both, smiles and yells down for Yedit to take. She locks off the rope by pulling it downwards with her brake hand and then walking backwards until it comes taut against Ilan's harness.

He looks around his little ledge: smooth, beautiful, gray-white stone, traced in red, scattered with needles from the cypress tree. Amazing. Yet, for some reason, he lacks the sense of achieving a likeness of Louis and of Yedit that ordinarily comes at the completion of a difficult climb. There's relief but no triumph. Confess it, the small voice demands, it wasn't Yedit you fucked on the counter that day. It was Anne. Yes, he confesses. Yedit had been too busy to leave her office, and then Anne had called to see how the house was coming. He asked if she wouldn't want to see for herself. She did. And she bought a thermos of vodka gimlets with her. And he pushed up her summer dress, pulled down her panties, and set her next to the stove.

Perhaps Yedit will let him go home now.

Ilan relaxes, lets go of the rock a second time, sits in his harness. Yedit slowly lowers him down the rock face. At last, his feet touch the ground. Louis claps him on the shoulder and hands him his carabiner full of tricams, two metal pyramids attached to long pink straps and a third attached to a red strap. He's killed a beautiful young woman and no one even seems to notice anymore. He's saved a café patio's clientele's worth of lives, including his own, and no one remembers. If only they balanced, or if not balanced, counted towards (or against) each other. They do not. They simply both are. Even he doesn't remember that he saved anyone particularly anymore. *If he'd invited her to sit for coffee. If they'd discussed her linguistics classes at the university. If they had fucked*. Obviously, he knows better, doesn't want to remember, obviously. If he were to occupy a role in the *Song of Songs*, it would be as one of the village guards who find the young lover alone in the city after dark and beat her.

"Tricams don't seem like the kind of thing you'd retire just because you dropped them," says Ilan.

"Nah. Nice climb by the way. Way to pull through."

"I shouldn't have had to take, and I shouldn't have freaked out."

"Gunks 5.9, man! Nothing to sniff at. Especially with an R+ rating and no gear. Listen, I'm going to take off, see if I can find something to set up on."

Yedit asks Louis if he wouldn't want to stay with them and top-rope the climb after she finishes with it. Ilan begins working open the knot tying him into his harness.

"It's your day."

Ilan wonders if Louis knows about that last time with Anne.

"It wouldn't be a big deal, right, Ilan? After all, we did nearly brain you with those tricams."

"You mean Ilan nearly brained me. Hey, I was the one who failed to wear a brain-bucket."

"I don't mind the extra time if Yedit doesn't, but after she cleans the pitch there'll be a nasty swing if you fall."

"That's appealing."

Yedit offers to leave a few select pieces of pro in place, and, while she lowers after completing the climb, to reclip them. Ilan rejects this suggestion on the grounds that Yedit's traverse back to the gear will be complicated, and might quite possibly fail, leaving expensive pro in the rock. Yedit, however, points out that she might not be able to complete the climb altogether. Gunks 5.9 is about her skill limit. It would be nice to have someone else who could follow her if she did not succeed.

"How about this? How about you clean the pitch, Yedit, rap off, and pull your rope. I'll hang out. If you succeed, maybe you guys can give me a quick belay while I lead it, by which time fucking Jesse should finally show up, and he can follow and clean for me. If you don't finish, I'll follow you and clean."

Jesse. Ilan has Yedit now. He doesn't need Louis to be his climbing partner. Doesn't even like climbing with Louis. Louis pushes him into and onto things he doesn't want to lead. Ilan has a Donna Karan vest with the outline of a bomb masked in tape on its lining. He has a beautiful wife. Jesse. Jesse and Louis and the way they are just back from that hike into the Wind River Range, and from the early season snows that meant tiptoeing across prematurely hair-trigger avalanche paths to pass into the Cirque of the Towers. Jesse probably didn't freak out during any of it.

If Yedit weren't here, Ilan might tell Louis he couldn't hang around. Yedit won't allow that though.

Ilan looks carefully at Louis. Somewhere in the man's head, Kashmiri separatists are still trying to flit across the border. Somewhere in the man's head, a chalkboard lists Indian and Pakistani cities; all of the Pakistani cities have lines drawn through them but only about half the Indian ones do: projected nuclear victory. Somewhere in the man's head, a switch has been turned to push and to strength and to constant burn in a way that Ilan can't quite seem to access for himself. And that he finds comfort in the fact that the plan means he won't have to climb for some period of time longer makes Ilan even more envious of whatever it is Louis has going on that lets him not mourn the people he's shot.

Ilan agrees to their belaying Louis after Yedit climbs, much as he wants the man away from him. Instead of kissing his wife after untying from the rope, Ilan sits on the ground, inserts his fingers in the heel-loops of his climbing shoes and peels them off.

This morning, while he beat eggs for omelets against the coffee maker's gurgling backdrop, Ilan told his wife that he thought he had gum disease.

"Gum disease?" Yedit asked.

"It aches around my teeth."

"When did you get so old?"

"I'm just saying my teeth hurt."

"When did you get so old?"

Yedit ties into her end of the rope, and Ilan pulls the slack out of his. The sweat down the back of his shirt begins to cool and chill him. He clips the rope into his belay device, smacks Yedit on the ass, toys with a smile, and she begins climbing. He betrayed her when they were renovating the house, didn't he. He betrayed Anne to be with Yedit, though too. He betrayed Israel by not being able to cope with killing the Palestinian woman and betrayed the Palestinian woman by shooting her. They say that when the Romans caught up with Rabbi Akiva, whose school was the foundry of the great givers of the Talmud, they raked him apart, literally combed the skin off his flesh, and the flesh off of his bones. And in the street beyond the walls of the courtyard in which they tortured him, passers could hear him scream, *Shema! Yisraeil! Adonai! Eloheinu! Adonai! Echad!* Ilan betrays God by being with Yedit; but when Ilan met Yedit, God had already betrayed him.

At the double-sloper where Ilan lost his shit, Yedit loses her grip and falls. He catches her on the top-rope easily. See, he thinks, I haven't betrayed her; I'm still strong on the rock.

And Akiva? Akiva left his wife to study Torah a double dozen years.

"Ain't a thing," he yells up.

She is on top-rope; nothing is at stake; her fall is harmless. Now she can't remind him of the paralyzing fear he suffered before reaching decent gear. She fell on top rope. If he'd fallen there, leading, he would have died.

Eventually, he figures, every couple must reach the point where certain equalizing failures make daily life tolerable. Nothing about feeling that way conflicts with wanting to support (or rather, outright supporting) one's partner. Two Thursdays ago, Yedit read from her book at the Chelsea Barnes and Noble, the large windowpanes reflecting a thick silent audience against a quiet Seventeenth Street night. He sat and waited for her to finish reading, then for her to finish signing, watched while young men flirted with her over open book jackets. An anemic few glanced back at him, perhaps wondering what this suited man was doing sitting in the last row of folding chairs, not seeking an autograph, long after most had left. They probably dismissed him as a stalkerish creep. No one would assume him her husband.

Yedit gets her hands back onto the rock and easily climbs past the slopers, yelling down to him what a hard move that was, that it caught her by surprise. Ilan begins to reply, but Louis says, "Damn straight that's a hard move. You're look great up there."

Ilan continues taking in slack as Yedit climbs and Louis continues to yell encouragement, staring—rather much, Ilan thinks—at Yedit's ass. Louis never yelled encouragement to Ilan. Ilan wonders whether that's a consequence of gender, or of his unique relationship with Louis. She easily reaches the roof, Ilan's few pieces of gear clipped to her harness now, where she rests for a moment. Ilan looks back out at the valley, disappointed that from the carriage road he cannot see the Hudson River cleaving the season's orange and yellow canopy. Climbing exhausts Ilan. Sure, all this is beautiful; but he's no longer certain that enduring the fear is a commodity fungible for commensurate self-confidence. You almost said the *Shema* up there, the small voice whispers.

He wonders whether he'll actually give the dollar to *tzedakah* now that he's down and safe.

Am I really so shallow, he thinks, as to damn my lover a heretic because she's more successful than me? Next time he comes back here, he will have to lead this without freaking out, or lead something harder, and so on and so forth, until the only solution is to walk around, a ticking bomb, ready to blow himself up and all around him. In truth, the climbing season can't end fast enough. For the first time in a long while, he wishes that he was at the office instead of the crag, and that he had plans to meet Anne at the Divine Bar after work for fancy glasses of wine, elaborate cocktails. He wants to sit and drink and not think. No, he corrects himself firmly, and the small voice is silent for a change. I want this life. String enough days together and we'll be ok. I love Yedit, he thinks. And a clap on his shoulder startles him from a fantasy of Yedit naked on her stomach, lying on the furs on the living room floor, his hand tracing her spine below her waist.

"Yo, yo."

Ilan turns. Jesse. Louis hugs him. Yedit resumes climbing and Ilan focuses on his belaying duties. A suspicion forms at the top of Ilan's chest and runs down his body until his bladder tingles and threatens to vacate into his ankle-chopped sweatpants. It's a suspicion that there was something else, or someone else, less fabulous, less beautiful even, who he met and passed by and cannot get back to. This mystery woman isn't Anne or, obviously, his wife. Don't tell me it's Dalia, Ilan preemptively replies to the small voice. He couldn't be with her if he couldn't be orthodox, certainly couldn't see her after sex with the orange-haired colonel.

A buried sense of a thing temporarily unneeded and thus forgotten percolates through Ilan's anxiety like a lost word whose concept can't quite be grasped until its syllables are annunciated. Its masked rising scares him into questioning whether his desperate attachment to Yedit isn't just that: a desperate attachment, an escape, an unfortunate entanglement best fled from. No, there was never an escape. He pulled the trigger and saved the café.

But Ilan...for Ilan, she finished her mission; for him, the bomb detonated. Hardware store sundries shattered and scattered him. His *neshama* ascended to learn Talmud full-time in heaven. And yet his *nephesh* is here, his body outlived his soul.

I need Yedit, Ilan murmurs. I love my wife. Thinking that he finally understands his paradox, Ilan finally understands his paradox: Yedit keeps him in contact with Louis; if she leaves him, he'll actually need Louis. But that's minor. The major thing, the opposition between Yedit and God, seems distant while he stands on the ground.

We're both reaching out, Louis and I, Ilan thinks, watching Louis laugh and preen for Jesse's amusement. Louis, a displaced Indian soldier, toughened in war, performs to impress a silly white American kid, a kid with brown dreads, a kid tall and anemic in a bean-fed New England waspy kind of way, the kind of kid who's righteous and carefree and paid for. Shuckling and jiving. Shucking, not *shuckling*, Ilan corrects himself. Shucking and jiving. *Shuckling* is what the men in synagogue do when they pray; it's the rocking back forth. And besides, Ilan muses, me, I'm clinging to a woman who's actually whole, beautiful, and successful, as if she could still be taken with me. There's nothing either of us can do to win these wars: we are who we are and they get to choose.

Yedit reaches the bolt anchors at the top of the climb and yells down to ask what she's doing.

"Clean and rap, baby!"

"Clean and rappel?"

"Clean and rappel!"

"Ok, take for a second."

The trail is still soft from the last of the morning's dew; and Ilan's footsteps leave clear depressions as he walks backwards to take up slack. He locks off the rope and leans back in his harness against its tension, anchored by Yedit's mass on its other end, on the far side of the anchor's pulley.

Louis and Jesse congratulate Yedit from the ground. Because she is married, because Ilan stands right there, they seem to feel it's ok to openly adore her. Ilan's mother's uncle, from the 'American side' of the family, lives in a Craftsman-style house in Red Bank, New Jersey. A few trees shelter it from its neighbors but allow sunlight onto the cabinets his uncle Mark built back in the Fifties when he homesteaded with the shiksa wife his parents accepted more than four decades ago. The American side of the family gathers there every several weeks, though they're older now, less able to travel, less able to drink vodka martinis garnished with jarred pearl onions and eat pasta and salad. That side of the family would no more consider rock climbing than joining a cult. They would no more mourn the Germans they shot in 'The War' than they would send their kids to private school. Ilan wonders whether he could ever raise a child, which reminds him of the old joke about the Jew who's stranded on a desert island. He proudly shows his rescuers the city he's built in the intervening years: Here's the butcher shop and this is the library and so on. They ask him, why two synagogues? Why two synagogues? He repeats, shocked. The one for which I *daven* in, and the one for which I wouldn't step foot inside, so help me the Almighty One, blessed be He. 'I belong to neither,' Ilan whispers to himself.

Louis turns from Jesse, "Are you talking to yourself, Ilan?"

"I thought you were shucking and jiving."

"What?" Louis asks.

Yedit yells, "Off belay!"

"Thank you!"

Ilan unscrews the locking gate on his belay carabiner and pulls the rope clear of his belay device. The slack end falls from his hands and swings to the ground.

"Belay is off!"

"Thank you!"

And that's that. Yedit will pull the rope through steel rings soldered onto the bolt hangars, clip in and rappel down. Since she seems super *gung ho* today, she'll probably want to lead the next few climbs. Ilan can relax. At this thought, he immediately, predictably, tenses inside, not wanting to see himself as afraid to lead more climbs and hence resentful of having to climb, now feeling that he'd much rather immerse himself in the busy life below the glistening towers an hour down-river.

Jesse and Louis walk over towards him, smiling.

They're leering fools, he thinks. They are no less pretentious than his counterparts downtown. Louis' maroon polypro zipper tee, Smith slider sunglasses, brown Carharrt work pants, La Sportiva approach shoes, hell, even his appropriately-scuffed rack of climbing gear, slung from a leopard-print Metolius sling, all of it—it all reflects a nuanced awareness of a particular culture's aesthetic prerequisites. He dresses to fit in, nothing more, nothing less. His savvy allows him to blend with his chosen peers despite his early career as a mountain soldier continents away. And yet, Louis will never be Jesse, never have what Jesse has. Ilan's no less dressed this way than Louis, either. Is this, then, Ilan's great escape from a world that respects most a man's ability to match a tie, buy a custom shirt, recognize a fine wine, teach a bartender how to fix a cocktail that later shows up on the bar's special-drinks board? Which wasn't that itself a great escape from a world that respects most a man's ability to protect with a gun? Though reducing Tel Aviv to only a culture of gun-fare is hardly fair.

A whispered "Fuck," the whistle of falling rope, all three turn, and at the *whump* of her body, the *whump* of her body, the *whump* of her body, the single, definitive sound of flesh on ground; Ilan falls to his knees.

Then he's crawling, stumbling to her, trying to gain his feet—only ten feet to go—and she, inert. The crowd rings him, gasps and swells with his approach of the body from beneath which, at once, blood pools out onto the carriage road, gravel islands jutting above the liquid surface.

Louis too, and Jesse, and the two women who've been climbing Horseman and are returning from the walk-off up the road for their packs, and somebody else, who seems to emerge from nowhere but insists on screaming that everyone stay back, give her room, and their dinner-guests from the prior weekend who've been climbing the stairs up from the lower parking lot, stairs that let out at the base of Apoplexy, and a jogger whose blue sports bra shows through her pink Lycra top, and a gust of rich soil that fills the nostrils with a mélange of humus and peat, and a mountain biker with his dog, and no one else, just these ten people, and amongst them, Ilan, who is no longer there, who stands in the center of a circle with the sun in the corner of his eyes as it peaks the treetops, him standing with a form that had once been his wife, but no longer moves. For a moment, he notices the purity of his focus, the singularity of his thought processes. Awareness taints his grief and he screams, the only part of his declaration that is made aloud is her name, but that declaration: Hear, oh God: "Yedit," my lord, "Yedit," my one! I choose "Yedit," God!

Someone, perhaps Louis, dispatches the mountain-biker to the ranger station.

The rope still hangs from the anchors Yedit had pulled it through before falling. It sways in the autumn light in the autumn breeze, a yellow-dappled blue line moving across sun-spotted white rock before disappearing up into golden-red tree crowns. Ilan, one leg crossed over the other in a sidestep around the form on the ground, still screaming in an attempt to remove the sense-memory of a rifle from his hands, touches a wisp of brown hair protruding from beneath her red helmet, freeing it to an errant breath of wind upon which it floats backwards. He smells earth.

Curled, face down, arms out.

A hand, perhaps Jesse's, reaches over Ilan's shoulder to finger her neck. Ilan feels the cold of that hand against his own flesh and shivers and slaps the hand away and puts his hand through her sweater's neck, reaches down to her breast, reaches to feel her heart's fluttering flutter. Before he can help himself, he knows that her bomb detonated when she published her book. There is no defusing her body, no reason for her not to survive.

"She has a pulse, a weak pulse."

But to believe, if for only a moment, in energy fields, or reiki, or prayer, or some other laying-on (or better yet, not laying-on) of the hands. To have some power, to move things, to change things, to affect the broken, dying body in front of you. Anything. Anything at all.

Then there are the racing people: The emergency workers, boards and straps and oxygen. There are the people to pull him back and away. There is a helicopter; there are the looks that they give him. There are the white medical jumpsuits of the men and women who leap from the helicopter and begin strapping his wife to the backboard and the crowd that has assembled and is dispersed. You are not a hero, Ilan thinks. You were never a hero. Though there is no danger of being treated as such, not this time. Louis silently drags him backwards ever backwards, further and further away. Jesse might demand to know where they are taking her, might scream into the white-clad body-workers condemning faces: which hospital will she go to? They might ride in a car, and from the car they might hear the blades of the life-flight ship in the air; and for once in his life Ilan might hear that rhythm of vertical flight, percussive as repeating mortars, and not think of long desert and men in khaki camouflage fatigues and the difference between Christians and Hezbollah and Jews.

Whatever there is, what is certain is that each incremental move draws him further from that silent body. Louis encourages him to speak. Louis encourages him to pray, which is a lie. Louis doesn't believe in prayer, which means Louis is being kind; Louis, considerate, which he never is. And all at once Ilan knows that he screams "Diti!" from the back seat of the car where Jesse holds him down and away from the door handles, where Ilan bites Jesse's wrist to attempt to break free.

There might be the suggestion that it is all about organ recovery, that his wife's last moments have acquired a different kind of value.

(Many years later, over a whiskey he shouldn't have drunk that followed a bunch of other whiskeys he should not have drunk, Ilan will explain to his newfound friend on the barstool beside him that if his wife hadn't agreed to donate her body, they might have flown her to a closer hospital—not that this would have saved her, she certainly would have died—but a shorter drive might have meant actually speaking to her while some something remained.

My wife translated, Ilan would explain: *And not from the desert mountains, no rising from the wilderness,* because the mountains came before the desert, Mt. Sinai before wandering in the Sinai. *Ki Elohim Shofet: Because the Lord judges; because the Lord is a judge.* And motioning downwards with a hand *zeh yashpil: This, He puts down; v'zeh: and this*—here, Ilan will pause to drink—*yarim.* Here, Ilan points to the sky. *And this, this He elevates.* Here Ilan will lift his glass. *Because there is a cup in God's hand,* or, as my wife also translated, *Because a cup in the hand of God, v'yayin chamar male meshekh.* Which, Ilan would explain to his besotted companion, might mean: *And foaming wine fills this mixed drink.* Or it might mean: *strict burning wine fills an evil mixture.* At which point Yedit asked what was meant by wine and what by mixture. *And he will pour out from this,* or, *And he will dwell and cause fear in this. Though dregs, they will find and they will drink all evil-of-the-world,* or, *Earth's sinners will find and will drink the dregs.*

She wrote, Ilan will proclaim: *Perhaps drinking from the cup God pours out makes you evil; perhaps the dregs are all that's left of the mixture when the evildoers finally reaches his cup. What's certain is that we drink what we find and we find what God pours and there's little choice in any of it but evil. He judges who rises up; He judges who gets put down, but mountains don't come from deserts.* She wrote the shit out of shit!

Ilan's companion will be disconcerted by the differing levels of drink in the two glasses before him, and by the fact that Ilan has poured a mostly full bottle of Budweiser onto the floor during this last.

Ilan will continue: His wife is dead, and yes, he would trade in however many lives her spare parts might save to secret between the folds of her fading consciousness a last reminder of himself. Then the bartender will take Ilan by the arm, lead him from his stool and his now-lost, new-found friend, lead him into the Manhattan night, but kindly. And a small voice will suggest: drunken man, did you want to tell her you loved her or hear her last confession of love for you?)

Part Two:

Same Day/Different Day

Ilan turns on his side to cradle his wife's back as she sits up, pulling the covers with her. Sun through the east-facing bedroom windows warms his eyelids, which he keeps shut as Yedit turns and runs her thumb along his cheekbone, a gesture that ends in her raking a stray hair out of his face and smoothing it down behind his ear. He continues to squeeze his eyes closed, to feign sleep, in the hope that she will continue to stroke his hair, kiss his cheek, trace his eyelids, anything, touch him. But Yedit stands; her feet plunk loudly onto the floor; the wide oak floorboards creak beneath her steps. He opens his eyes and props himself up on one elbow to face her back. She continues to tiptoe across the room, her shoulders bunched and her arms crossed in front of her. Her spine's accentuated line descends from the slope of her long hair, which drapes around the side of her neck and in front of her right shoulder.

Ilan can visualize her skeleton, the flesh boiled away from the bones, her hair made into a wig, her perfect architecture the eerie trophy of an Eastern European professor's office. Yes, he thinks, the Nazis would have killed her too. But they would have saved her structure. She's too beautiful for the gas chambers and the crematoria; for her there would be injections and preservation. Before this image a vacuum of powerlessness swells beneath Ilan's thoughts. Yedit, he thinks, is the unknowable beauty of a biblical Sarah. But that would not have protected her. What matters the manner of killing? Concoctions, explosive concoctions, shrapnel made of household hardware, randomness: These are life; these are death. There is no control, no ascendancy, no God. I can't even choose whether to keep or lose her, Ilan realizes horrified, awestruck. Quickly, a small voice commands, focus on her body. The corporeal will save you.

Her hips shift as she steps forward and the flat triangle at the bottom of her spine reminds him of the line from *Nine and a Half Weeks*: "Have you ever had a girl with a heart-shaped ass?" And Ilan wonders what his wife would look like dressed in a tux and top hat, drinking wine with him down at Harry's on Hanover Square.

"Where ya going, Diti?"

"To the boudoir, Lani. I'm cold. I'm getting a robe."

"It's not a boudoir, love. A boudoir is a bedroom; that is a wardrobe."

"Thanks for the French lesson."

"*Bevakasha*."

Yedit turns and curtsies, her chilled nipples arcing down then back up. Ilan thinks about biting them, lightly, about how her back would arch, just enough for him to sling an arm around her waist. She opens the antique wooden doors and takes out a blue silk robe. The elbows are practically worn through and the gold embroidery sprouts loose threads. She used to have an old canvas work shirt of her father's as well, but that finally wore out. He sighs and tries to imagine getting out of bed. His mouth is dry and his head muffled. They drank some of Louis' home-made wine last night. Ilan gasps, shuts his eyes again; an incandescent-lit image of his kitchen, of himself quoting Louis' opinions about nuclear war on the Asian subcontinent back at Louis.

Ilan reopens his eyes in time to watch Yedit leave the room.

Ilan mutters, "Oh, God," to himself and turns his face back into his pillow. He thinks he can smell a trace of bile in the eight-hundred-count Egyptian cotton and wonders for a moment whether he puked. He didn't puke. He didn't drink all that much.

A few glasses of wine, that's it. He murmurs, "Fuck," over and over to himself; a meditative curse, he thinks. (As if it was the one night, as if a drink could be blamed.) He sits up and his spine's creak remembers the way the sun struck Anne's bed the second Sunday he woke up there. The sheets, raw and soft, anchored him further into her queen-sized mattress, the bed quite nearly filling every inch of the small East Village bedroom she'd crammed it into more by alchemy than geometry. He curled his toes and stretched his legs. Eyes still closed, the cotton telegraphed up through his stiff calves and hamstrings. Something dark and warm blotted the sunlight. He could almost feel skin along his chest. "Drink" she commanded.

When he opened his eyes, the flute full of mimosa sparkled like an Architectural Digest centerfold.

Ilan sighs and forces himself out of bed. This is how it goes: He takes a day off work to climb with his wife. His hated best friend shows up with a bottle of homemade wine the evening prior. To prove something, and because he doesn't have to work the next day, he has a glass or two—that despite three years' sobriety. Now he wishes he could sleep in or go to work—everything sounds better than goading himself into leading climbs that scare him to impress his overly-impressive wife.

A pause in Yedit's footsteps interrupts his thoughts.

There's a spot on the staircase where the murky projections of warped glass through an original eight-paned window warm a few steps. He's watched her stop there, stretch out her arms and bathe in the sun, slowly spinning, lowering her head to let the light warm her neck.

He begins to move, tiptoes, hoping to catch her at it, spinning, lost in the sun. She claims she's changed her methodology, begun studying Stanislavski's system, method acting, as a way of entering the writer's she translates. Ilan supposes that one need only understand the angry fear of a beseeching child to emulate the speakers of the psalms. For the *Song of Songs*, Yedit has begun trying to imagine her way into Solomon, into his wives. I am the speaker of the psalms, Ilan thinks and then rejects. The psalms' speakers believe in God. Not the way your wife translates them, they don't, a small voice chides. "They do believe; they just can't quite access Him. They've lost the knack of asking Him to be Him," Ilan whispers to himself, slip-sliding on tiptoes across the floor, and wonders whether his wife realized this nuance when she wrote that translation.

He reaches the top of the stairs and catches a glimpse of her lowering her arms. She stays in the spot though, facing east, arms by her side, legs together. The stance in which one recites the *Amidah*, the prayer that replaces the thrice-daily sacrifices made in the Bait-Migdash. He starts down. Perhaps, he hopes, she's waiting for him to catch up. His right foot hits the top stair; it creaks; and she starts walking down again.

"Omelets sound good, Diti?" he yells after her.

"Whatever."

"Climbing food, yeah?"

She hurries off down the steps and he lags behind her, ungainly weighting each successive step in turn.

"Are you mad because I had some of Louis' wine last night?"

No answer.

He finds her sitting on a stool, her head on her arms on the blue and orange tile surface of the kitchen island. He stops, sensing dead Israeli kings in the room, his wife's muttered longings to play Cleopatra to a man with a thousand wives.

Ilan moves his hands as if to touch her, though she's much too far away.

He approaches, opens his mouth to speak, says nothing.

He comes closer to her and she lifts her red wet eyes.

Ilan suppresses a smile at the strange childishness of this face that is otherwise so desperately mature, beautiful, adult: She's a professor! A scholar! A woman who looks *senior* to her students! Senior to her colleagues, even! But her lips tremble, her mouth half open, her hair mussed, her robe too big. Lost uncertainty. Child-like. Somewhat comical. Cute.

He can taste the goose bumps beneath her nipples in the tickle on his tongue—if she would run her fingers into his scalp and push his head down her body—

"I can't, Ilan. I just can't anymore."

"Can't what, baby?"

His voice soft, modulated, smoothed out, purposefully gentle. The wild rush of impending disaster replaces his desire to smile, the carefree, adrenalin-fueled, what-me-worry that comes with the decision to get on a hard, really hard climb. But her robe, partially open, draws his attention to the wedge of exposed breast, oddly shaped, rounded, ruddy like a summer snowfield bounded by lichen-blued boulders. He knows that beneath the breakfast bar her crossed legs split the robe's lower hem in a similar triangle. What would it mean, Ilan wonders, to be King Solomon and to covertly woo? Why go meet this thousandth-and-one wife in the streets of the city at the risk of its guards?

For thighs, Ilan answers himself, her inner thighs. But dryness leaks from his eyes and wilts the corners of his smile, the smile he no longer desires. Come on, he chides himself, rally. This is what's been coming a long time now!

One stupid drink and she 'can't' anymore.

Don't be an asshole, asshole; it's not the fucking drink. For once his chest tingles without the Palestinian woman walking towards him.

"Can't this. Can't this anymore, Ilan." She bangs the flat of her hand on the countertop. She tilts her head on its side. "Come on. Please."

This must be very hard for her, whatever she's going through: the fucking book. And the fucking new book. Tehillim and now Solomon: father and son, if you think about it. Ilan looks at his hands: they're small; they're weak. Would he rather his wife not be successful? Wishing he wasn't speaking out loud, he asks, "Is there something between you and Louis?"

What he doesn't ask is whether she's looked through the browser history on his laptop. He doesn't ask whether she's discovered his new compulsion, his research, his investigation. It's always seemed self-evident that those who wished to—especially in a country as open as America—could get whatever explosive materials they wished. Television shows depict sweaty swarthy men making backroom deals for missing military explosives. But Ilan wanted to know whether someone like him, someone without connections, someone who would be an easy mark for government undercover agents—should he even know who to ask about who to ask to find one of those—could make a bomb. At first, he focused on obvious explosives meant for innocuous uses: firecrackers, model rocket engines, black powder, fuel. All of these seemed possible, yet dismissible.

Then he remembered the incident report the orange-haired colonel had given him. He'd waited a day to call her back after she'd left his apartment. She had told him that his weakness disgusted her. Then she sighed, confessed that she shouldn't have slept with him. 'No,' he'd protested. 'That was great. Can we again?' She'd paused on the phone. Then she'd told him she was going to send him something that would help, but that he shouldn't call again. It took him two days searching his old files to remember that he'd folded the pages into the leather-bound prayer-book his family's Pittsburgh congregation had given him for his bar mitzvah.

On the bomb squad's section of the report he found, *imah shel satan*. Mother of Satan, he translated. He found it online easily enough. Triacetone triperoxide. Made up of household ingredients. Hydrogen peroxide, paint thinner, and car battery acid. But just knowing the ingredients is like knowing that humans are made of water, iron, carbon and calcium. And so more research, more exploration; and Ilan's curiosity, aided by a rudimentary understanding of Arabic, brought him closer and closer to an intellectual understanding, a theory, if you will, of almost-stable homemade explosive powder, slim enough to conceal in a vest with room left over for screws and nuts, wire and scrap metal.

All of that stays at the back of his mind, a minor cloud that one day may rain. Meanwhile, the improbable conclusion that his hated best friend has begun fucking his wife leads him to inquiries he regrets faster than he can utter them.

Ilan is living a fucking cliché. His wife is upset and so he assumes that she's having an affair, naturally, and with the most recent available man they've seen, based on nothing more than her distress and the man's recent proximity. And also on Louis being Louis. Which is to say that Ilan wonders whether Louis might not fuck Yedit just to get Ilan to start drinking and mountaineering again. Would Louis really ruin Ilan's marriage to have Ilan back as a climbing partner? It's unthinkable and flattering and distinctly possible.

He looks at his wife.

She chokes on her laugh.

Wouldn't Louis, Ilan worries, choose Yedit over him if their marriage failed?

Yedit coughs, says, "Oh, Ilan. No. There's nothing between me and anyone. Certainly not Louis."

"If certainly not Louis, then who possibly?"

"Ilan. Please."

"Do you want to see other people?"

"Stop."

"Then what is the 'this' that you can't do?" Still with the carefully modulated voice, the intense quiet seriousness, the conscious reflection of potential hurt, of dignity and fragility. He hates himself, Ilan does. He's fucking despicable, fucking pathetic.

"This, this going on this way."

"You're not telling me anything."

"I am. You refuse to listen."

"Listen? All I hear is 'this' and 'can't' and 'anymore' as if there's been some abstract hell to which I've persisted in confining you for some indefinite but certainly protractedly long period of time. What am I supposed to do with that, Diti? What the fuck do you want me to do?"

"Oh don't be an asshole."

"Do you want me to go to counseling? I'll go. Do you want us to go together? I'll do that too. Anything you want."

"I don't want you to just do anything I want, Ilan."

"You know, fuck you."

He turns away from her, from the control and dismissal in her voice. He takes down a pan from the cabinet, eggs, butter, and cheese out of the fridge. While turning the flame to medium on one of the Viking range's seven burners, he repents his explicative to her over his shoulder.

"I think it's what you want, Ilan. It frees you, my leaving."

"That's crap."

"I don't care that you're an asshole. I don't care that you can't stand my independence. Whatever. You're a man. It's the other thing, the one you can't say, that I can't say for you."

"Enough with the goddamn mystery. Just tell me what the fucking problem is."

She doesn't answer. He bought the fucking stove for her, after all. The whole fucking kitchen. The house. Everything. Her life. True, she doesn't cook. But he could cook on any level surface with a gas flame. Do they need this? He turns the cheese over in his hand before selecting a Tojiro chef's knife from the magnetic strip and cutting slices for their omelets. And yet there is a convenience. The comfort of Cookie-Monster slippers and fleece throws and thick white carpeting. The comfort of hibernation and mediocrity. The middle ground between enormous wealth and the ability to physically sense one's surroundings itches in Ilan's gullet. Asshole, he tells himself. Stop being so fucking dramatic. You're not an angsty eighteen-year-old anymore. But then he never was. In the IDF it simply wasn't an available category of being. And once something proves incapable of persistence in one setting, it never feels organic anywhere again.

"Is there something we can do to make this better, Yedit?"

"I don't know."

She's so quiet, her voice so very quiet. A whisper. A non-sound. The respectful hush of worshippers in front of something extraordinarily large. Ilan chops a thick chunk of butter with a decisive, downwards, knife thrust. He has an image of his own strength, of himself as a hero of sorts. But I'm cutting butter, he bitterly chides, butter! He almost whispers the disgusting word aloud as he tosses the piece into the hot pan where it rolls around leaving melt streaks like comet tails.

He waits a minute.

They aren't looking at each other, haven't since he began cooking. He can hear her breath, the slight tear-congested catch in her inhale. Then, with the pan nearly too hot, he remembers to beat the eggs. There is the sound of the whisk cutting through yolk to scrape the metal bowl's bottom. He pours the whipped eggs into the pan. The mixture's edges harden.

"Fuck me!" Ilan curses.

"What, Ilan?"

"I forgot the Herbs de Provence."

"Ugh."

"What ugh?" Ilan turns and faces his wife.

"Ugh, ugh."

He turns back to the pan. He could sprinkle the herbs into the congealing egg. They'll stick together in clumps, little clusters of trees, gardens. Better to leave well enough alone.

"Do you want out, Yedit?"

A loud sob crosses the counter at his back, then another and another. Real crying. Ilan looks up at the steel-clad splatter guard behind the stove. There was a time when it appeared Yedit might not get tenure. None of the academic publishers were particularly interested in what they viewed as an essentially creative work. As her book failed to find a home, her colleagues, once enamored of her seemingly radical revision of what it meant to be an academic, an exegetist, began to question whether she was actually a scholar. Back then, when she was forced to show at her cramped office on campus, making herself visible to ever-vigilant, ever-skeptical senior faculty, she needed Ilan. She would come home beaten, uninspired, tearful. Back then he was a full person in this marriage.

"You used to be so—" she says, through tears.

"Fucking drunk," Ilan cuts in.

She starts to shake her head, no, and then rolls her eyes upwards and shakes her hands beside her face instead.

She does care, he tells himself. The line from the *Song of Songs*, *Yonek shadey imi*,[8] comes to him, *a child at my mother's breasts*. 'Could the transgression in the song be that of incest?' Yedit wondered aloud one afternoon in their backyard, 'her lament: *oh, that you had to be like a brother for me, a child at my mother's breasts!*' Yedit slowly reading, sucking on something tall, cold and alcoholic that Ilan had garnished with a cucumber slice. He sat next to her, going over account paperwork for something to do, Fresca in his glass. Or is it a wish, a hope that the transposition of her mother's breasts for her own will erase the desire to have him on her? Incest, well that begs the reversal, if love is taboo because it happens between siblings, then don't lovers eventually become as brother and sister? No, I cannot be your brother, Ilan thinks at the silent woman across the breakfast bar. I will not, I will absolutely not be as a brother to you. I am your husband. I fuck your vagina. This last internal outburst sets his lower lip to trembling. Really? the small voice reminds him. You make fancy cocktails for your wife even though you're not allowed to taste them. I had to sober up to be with her, he whispers. You were free, you made your own choices, the small voice persists. He shuts it up by asking aloud, "How could you not want me to be willing to do anything for you?"

She doesn't answer and he shouts, "How?"

No answer and the sobs come and go like an afternoon thunderstorm that threatens and threatens to blow over, each pause prelude to repetition. More rain and more rain still.

You think you can help her with Shlomo's song? Ilan asks himself, his thoughts suddenly as calm as if he were sipping campfire tea while waiting out mountain weather. If you shared a breast when you were but sprouts, then she could kiss you in the street without drawing notice. Why no notice? Can a wife not kiss a husband?

Yedit's a person, Ilan thinks, a human, a woman that you love. But the crowd of people, of men, around her when Vassar hosted her book-signing last year. Men, a crowd of them, that he could not push through. And he imagines himself the Palestinian woman's husband outside the ring of onlookers and security, trying to push through to the black form, the shattered angles of coat and concrete oozing woman. So Ilan was inside one ring and outside another. But she's a person, Ilan thinks, and then asks: which is a person? Yedit? The one he shot? His eyes open wide, still fixed on the intersection of the diagonal creases in the backsplash, his locked elbows trembling under his weight. There's no escape is there, he thinks, wondering whether he hasn't whispered aloud after all.

A sounds percolates from between the sobs, hardly spoken at all, like the crack of dark damp life deep in a slot canyon beneath a desert. Ilan struggles to decode what she's said. He thinks she's said: "I don't know."

He drops sliced cheese into the omelet and spatules it closed. Ilan turns around. His wife sniffles, snorts, exhales, sighs, wipes a hand across her nose, huffs. Whispers that she's sorry.

"Sorry doesn't sound like you don't know."

"I'm so sorry."

If he rescued her cheeks from her tears, would their luster would be lost like river rocks brought to dry land?

"Diti, let's us try to fix this."

"Ok."

He turns back to the omelet, flips it, tells his wife he loves her, asks her if they shouldn't go climbing, puts the omelet on a plate; and before he can hand her breakfast, she's opened her mouth again and left him. He sets the plate before her anyway, crosses his arms over his chest and asks if she's sure.

She nods and repeats that she is sorry.

He looks at her omelet. Hexagons of light refracted through her orange juice glass point away from the sunroom's windows. That the eggs are the same yellow as the flower pattern that borders their plate makes the plate seem new despite the chip off of its edge; makes the whole thing look staged: not breakfast but a photo-shoot of breakfast. He should have dumped it in her lap.

"Is this what you really want?"

She stage whispers, "Yes!" Tints it with exasperation.

"Well if what you want is out, and you're getting out, then why are you crying?"

"Oh, baby. Don't, just don't. Please."

Yedit throws her hands up and tilts her head back to the side again. Ilan touches his cheek. No, he isn't crying. Why did he ever give up drinking? Why did he stop being the person who met Yedit at a climbing gym a few months after she'd moved to the city and invited her out for a glass of wine the next night at the Divine Bar? How? When? That night turned into two bottles of '96 Pesquera. A hundred and forty bucks in wine, another seventy in food—and he didn't even get laid. A couple of kisses over the low table separating their lounge chairs and an impassioned walk up Broadway, hand in hand, bright eyes and ear nips. Why did he ever leave the Upper East Side for this house in the country?

Blah, blah, blah, asshole, he thinks, and if you hadn't met her you'd be a few years out from your first bypass or something like that. And another voice whispers quietly, if you hadn't met her you never would have watched the psalms twinkle like bubbles blown from a child's wand.

It's simple, he thinks. I love what I can't have. As she grows distant, I love her more. As I love her more, I grow weaker. As I grow weaker, I lose the power to keep her. Oh snap out of it, he commands himself; and the small voice suggests, you love God then, too, because you can't have Him.

"You're sure you're not seeing anyone?" Ilan asks.

"No."

"I don't understand."

"How can you not understand?"

"Do you love me?"

"How could you ask that?"

"Well?"

Ilan shakes his head and notices that the kitchen smells like coffee, which reminds him that they own a coffee-maker with a timer, that last night he set that timer after grinding beans, filling the basket and loading the water reservoir, all in the expectation that he and Yedit would wake up to the smell of coffee, make a quick breakfast, and then go climbing. He always meets her with coffee. When they were first dating, he would call her early, six in the morning, wake her up and tell her to be outside in twenty minutes. And there she'd be when he arrived in his black Lexus. Her hair wet, the Tehillim tucked under her elbow. Ilan pours himself a cup of coffee, sighs, and then pours a cup for Yedit as well.

Sipping his coffee, he walks towards Yedit. Bitter warmth sinks through his digestive tract, peeling him open from the inside. He sets her cup down in front of her and looks out the kitchen window.

Flagstone extends from the house before giving way to overgrown grass, frost covering its seeded tops. Burnt red brush and wild blueberries buffer the grass from violently yellow-leafed woods. From within the trees' shadows a brown shape conforms into a slow-walking doe, as casual as a dairy cow. She steps from the tree line into the brambles and stops, cocking her head so one fixed eye faces the window. Silently, first one, then two, then three gangly, near-grown fawn follow her and likewise stop, their legs spread way far apart, awkwardly angled, unstable.

Ilan lifts his cup to point them out to Yedit. But the action limits his focus to the kitchen again, and he sets the mug back down, ceramic against tile, and sighs.

Yedit sips her coffee.

She's left him not moments ago and yet she thinks nothing of sitting across from him at the kitchen counter he paid for, of his making her coffee, of sipping it with such goddamn...Act on that and you won't win her back, he thinks. And what will win her back? He can't answer the question. Nor can he decide whether he'd rather be vengeful now, treat her leaving as a done deal, or continue to operate within the confines of their marriage.

For two months of spring Sundays, as the botanical gardens slowly came into bloom, Ilan leveraged his relationship with the Director of Member Services, a client (short term paper), to take Yedit into the gardens an hour before they opened. They would tour the Japanese gardens, the roses and the coy ponds, before landing on the lawn beneath the cherry trees as the gates opened to the regular public. There, she would slowly translate the Tehillim for him, a psalm or two each week, explaining the redundancies in the Hebrew, the balancing of terms and phrases, the Ugaritic roots of

Baal, God of the weather, and the deities of streams and earth. She would dream for him how her translations of Tehillim and Job, once complete, would earn her tenure.

Outside, the deer wander into the center of the lawn's bramble-border and dip their heads, front legs spread wide, to graze. Whoever lives in the house next will probably plant gardens, which the deer will raid, sabotage. This will lead them to build a fence, and that fence will invariably be a tall wooden one, probably white picket, to match the structure.

The house, fortified, retreats from Ilan, and, in turn, the life he has finally been able to barely grasp with the tips of his fingers, nails scraping down his wife's beautiful sides as he falls off and plummets back into his old self.

"Fuck. Louis bringing that wine over...what was that? What was I thinking?"

"You had a couple of glasses of wine. So fucking what."

"So fucking what? What, it's ok for me to drink now? I should start drinking again?"

"No. Ilan. Sure, whatever. Drink, don't drink. I don't care."

I did my part, Ilan hopes he hasn't said aloud. I killed one woman and abandoned my vices for another. Shouldn't I have some peace now?

They hopscotched the gardens that budding spring, a new quadrant in full bloom each week, the sun brighter and earlier and warmer with every visit. Their second time there, Ilan's client insisted they tour the greenhouse's blooming orchids. Void of humans, the dank jungle—coned orange flowers stretching towards algae-hazed panes, humid perfumes that hinted at worn underwear and midtown midday tea-rooms, lush with nineteenth-century reproduction brocades and withered wealthy forearms jangling opal-chained watches and gold hoop bracelets, red vines creeping along gravel walkways, an echo with no source sound—seemed as if it should tempt them towards hide-and-seek, horseplay. The orchids themselves were behind glass in a giant case in the northeast corner of the building. Yedit leaned forward till her face was against the pane. Ilan rested a hand on the small of her back and leaned with her.

"Clinical," she said.

"Not so loudly."

"Parasitic."

He absentmindedly rubbed her back and suggested they go outside.

"Thank you. Let's."

They left the building and wandered past rows of flowering shrubs still covered with burlap and wicker. Yes, this, Ilan thought. I am resilient. It is the martyr who ends on the ground with my bullet in her. I go on. They destroy the building across the street from my office, but I survive. I get out. I am powerful. I am power. I am the one who brings a beautiful woman to a beautiful garden before anyone is allowed in. He leaned forward and whispered into the elegantly rounded edge of Yedit's ear how amazing these gardens were in the heart of Brooklyn, the not-particularly-nice part of Brooklyn.

"*Kol kach yafe*," she whispered back. And birds singing, or fighting, attracted their attention to a grove of short thick spruce. "They're so green."

"Look down."

She commented that the lightly-lavender crocuses weaving around the uneven sides of white and gray stones were also beautiful but she did not drop to her knees and fondle them, or gasp, or swoon. When Gideon wanted to thin his army, he told them to drink at a stream. Those that put their mouths to flowing water he cut; those that scooped up water in their hands and drank while continuing on he kept. Ilan crouched down carefully, pulling up his trouser legs at the thighs. He cupped one of the blossoms between his middle and ring fingers. Make her swoon, he silently commanded the yellow stamen. Why do you need her to swoon? He thought. He let go of the flower.

"They'll open the gates soon," he said.

"Shall we go to the cherry trees?"

He didn't answer her but stood and held out the crook of his elbow. She took it for a moment, let him lead her. Together, not talking, they walked to the lawn. There were enough leaves on the closest tree to block the sun mostly, but when he looked at a new bud on the crown's periphery, a halo of light turned the closed white petals and purple traced sepal into a red-rimmed black ball. He blinked and saw spots, muttered to himself, then plopped down beneath the offending tree.

"Well at least we're here first."

She sat down at his feet and began to read softly, without translating. For a while, he tried to hang onto his distemper, focusing his angst on a Chasidic couple pushing a double stroller. Breeders. His parents may have been orthodox but at least they were modern, clean. But the psalms' words kept coming and the couple quite nearly became a phrase. Dovid would sing for them, he thought, who am I to begrudge them the lawn, the trees, the sun, the sky? Yedit sat at his feet and read.

It's been a long time since they've gone to the gardens, Ilan thinks. There's been an exchange: Cultivation for the Gunks' natural beauty; himself as Yedit's only audience for a true public; and in his sense of loss, Ilan's ears prickle with suspicion of his emasculation. He tries to cut off the whisper—You couldn't even really handle killing your enemy—that threatens the stillness with which he gazes at his traitorous wife. The whisper, the small voice, the chiding continues: You were too much of a coward to deal with a necessary killing. And now what, you're researching explosives? Do you want to be caught? No one will catch you. So you'll move out of internet research and into experimentation. You'll use cash instead of credit cards to purchase antiseptic and car batteries and paint thinner. It will be easier without a snooping wife to convert your bucolic back yard, your clearing in the woods, into an explosives proving ground.

"Diti, do you remember on our first trip to Quebec how beautiful the plants were above tree-line in the Grand Jardin?"

"I remember walking beneath a lot of giant power lines coming from the Hudson Bay."

"But surely."

"Surely you realize that the framed photo next to the bathroom door is reminder enough."

"We should have gone back and climbed some of those granite faces."

"And you would lead those routes? It's not like there are guidebooks, or chalk highways up the rock."

"I've made first ascents."

"You've accompanied Louis on first ascents."

"Why the fuck would you compare me to him, Yedit?"

"I'm not mad at you."

"Then what is it?"

"You know what it is."

"Just say it."

"You can't believe in me and God both."

"That's not an answer."

"I don't believe I said that it was."

"I don't believe in God."

On the third or fourth of those spring Sundays in the Garden, Ilan looked over at Yedit. They lay perpendicular to each other on the grass and his head wasn't far from her stomach. Her white blouse had shifted up, exposing her navel. In nearly a month of spending time together, he had never taken her shirt off, nor seen her in the evening (excluding, of course, their initial tryst at the Divine Bar, during which she had explained her arrival in New York, which was her departure from Boston, how after defending her dissertation to a committee formed jointly between Harvard and the Jewish Seminary, a dissertation that leveraged Rashi and Ramban to untangle an historical exegesis of the Exodus story, something about the Golden Calf not being a false god so much as a false method of summoning an invisible and abstract deity, she found herself teaching composition as an adjunct at Boston College. When Vassar offered her a job, it was as if firmament had risen upon the waters. She left her life and her friends and moved to New York City).

Her abdomen was smooth with a thin line of muscle definition circling its upper half. She lay on her side with her back facing east and the rising sun seemed to bend around her and cast a glow along the border of her flesh. Ilan placed a hand flat on her stomach. It was warm and soft. Where his forearm emerged into sunlight, the shadows of leaves waved along his arm, a monochrome Klimt-pattern of dark and light projected on his skin. She stopped reading; her breath quickened pace.

Keep going, he told her.

She resumed: *Lulei adonoi shehayah lanu, bikum alenu adam.* He could feel the words in her belly, and moved his face against it. She gasped softly at the feel of his cheek. For a moment, he didn't bother to comprehend the words, just felt the consonant blocks of Hebrew and English flowing down through her body, melding with his face and the grass and the sun and the cherry trees, whose blossoms, temporarily stalled by a freshet of cold weather, had not yet opened, but would soon, now that it was warm. *Azay hamayim shitfunu, nachlah, avar al-naphshenu.* His face against her side, his hand still there as well: he could feel tension flood through his own body, desire vibrate out of her reading and into him: *Because without you... the flood waters would have washed past our souls*[9].

He kissed her stomach, wrapped his arms around her body, slowly swam her. Her reading tapered. Her eyes closed. Her head tilted back. From her neck oatmeal and lavender from her body scrub barely masked a hint of her smell, date pollen on a saltwater breeze. He kissed her breasts through her shirt, her clavicle, her long unbroken bow of trachea. And he thought, if women swoon in men's arms, then this is swoon, because he could feel her collapse into gravity, the ground warping with blood flushing his brain, his balance bent, though they both lay on firm earth, on soil, unchanging, the tip of a great moraine forced out to sea in the last ice age by the Wisconsin sheet, now exposed to the sun. He could feel the possibility of fall beneath them in the swirling eruptions of his own mental chemistry.

"Then to our souls would have flowed the breaching succession. Diti. I love you."

"Kigamul aley imo, kagamool alay naphshi: Like a child finished, a weaned one upon his mother, so sated upon me is my soul. Finished from my soul[10]. Weaned. Prepared to go on."

"Do you know..." He starts, ready to tell about his boss and the bathroom, the vomiting and the web-surfing at work. Instead, he says, "I feel like I maybe can't control my thoughts."

"Control them." Yedit cautions.

"No, not that kind of thought."

"I don't care."

"I keep seeing the woman I shot in Tel Aviv."

"Is that a threat?"

"Of what? Yedit. No. I'm saying it's been starting again. The images. The compulsions. The sense of..." Ilan stops himself before saying, God, "The sense of something."

Yedit visibly recoils, says, "That's so unfair, Ilan."

"What about translating the *Shema*? Instead of the *Song of Songs*?"

Yedit makes a noise that Ilan has never heard before. Something between a sneer and the sound of vomiting. "Go back to the shtetl, Ilan. Repent. They'll find you a new wife. One that keeps her head covered."

"So this is about the tefillin last week."

"Jesus Christ."

"I told you, I was looking through my old files and found them. I wanted to see if I remembered how."

"Remembered how?"

"Yes."

"How what? How to wrap leather straps around your arms and your head so that you can pray?"

"I wasn't praying."

"Only spelling God's name on your arm with leather straps."

"When Moses was on Sinai he only saw God's tefillin knot."

"You're telling me biblical history, Ilan. Me."

"I can contribute. We could collaborate."

"On the *Shema*? Yeah. I'll consider that."

Ilan cups his mug with both hands. Going back to bed would be nice. Or maybe he should go into the office after all. Past Yedit's shoulder, the doe raises her head sharply, her ears cocked. The faun belatedly follows its mother's lead, lifting its head as well. Ilan blinks. Yedit's stare, now clear and focused, tingles along his forehead. She slides her hands between the coffee cup and his palms. She cares, sure, but it feels condescending. He looks away from her to show that he's hurt and in the periphery of his vision the out-of-focus forms of mother and baby deer sprint for the sheltering trees.

Two years ago, when Yedit finally turned away from the scholastic options for her book's publication, and submitted it to an ordinary literary agent, Ilan brought her a new pack filled with new gear and announced that they would traverse the Presidential Range from north to south. "In winter?" Yedit wondered.

"Exactly." Ilan replied.

Yedit smiled and put her hand flat on his chest. "And what about your work?" she asked, stepping into him.

He assured her that he'd arranged coverage for the week.

"And if the agent calls?"

"If she calls, she wants you. If she wants you, she'll wait."

"She'll wait."

"I would wait for you," he said.

Yedit, so close that her breast pressed against her hands that were still on his chest, whispered into his ear that she would do anything for him.

"Then," he said, "Get in the car. Your bag's already packed."

When he woke up next to the orange-haired colonel, his sleep-sweat had stained his form into the sheets. He rolled towards her, moving from his frightened damp. Shivering, he held on to her. Her back arched away from his wet stomach and she broke free from him. Sat up. Arms wrapped around his chest, teeth chattering, he watched her pull her bra over her breasts, snapping the shoulder elastic into place, and then step into her panties, back bent, one leg at a time. He wished he had the strength to stand up and walk behind her. He wished he could hold her again, taste the folds of her labia. The lace top of her floral briefs adjusted, she stood upright and narrowed her green eyes at him. His admiration of the ridges and muscles of her abdomen tasted of fever and rotten oranges. Ilan stared, unspeaking; the colonel made a noise, pulled on her slacks and shirt, grabbed her purse and left.

Ilan presses Yedit's hand against the coffee mug and tries to focus on his wife. Should he be nice? Should he buy her flowers? Should he point out that she lives in a house he paid for, surrounded by possessions he bought her, in a life he largely facilitated and introduced her to? Should he offer to change? Offer to go back to counseling?

"Ilan, I have to go. This isn't working for either of us. It's killing you. Let me go."

"Don't judge what's right for me. For me, I would defend our marriage."

"Then for me. I need to go."

"Ok."

"Thank you."

"Where will you go?"

Ilan removes his hands and takes his coffee cup. And after the coffee's finished, how will you occupy yourself? he thinks, parsing his sips. If only there was some action, some activity to occupy him. Yedit drags her hands back to her own cup. She lifts it to her mouth but instead of actually drinking, blows ripples on its surface.

"The coffee's cool enough to drink, Yedit."

"I hadn't thought about where I would go yet."

Ilan finishes his last drips. His anxiety shifts into his bowels before Yedit's slack-faced stare. Remember this, Ilan, he thinks, her look, because later, when the other kinds of thoughts set in, and you want to believe that she used you, or that she moved on from you, or that she never really loved you—then you can remember this look and know that this wasn't a happy moment in her life either.

He catches a glimpse of his romantic future, of meeting someone after a time, of having to explain to them all his weird quirks, his history in the Israeli army, the shooting, his tormented desire for a God in which he has no faith. It seems so exhausting. How, the small voice asks, will you explain your research into bomb-making? Maybe, he thinks, I won't have to. You mean, the small voice asks, you don't plan to actually a build a bomb? Of course not, Ilan yells at the voice. Then how, the voice continues, will you ever know if the authorities would manage to stop you in time? I'm the authorities, Ilan responds, I happen to notice at the last minute and pull the trigger. Sure, the voice sneers, that worked out great.

Angry at the voice, at himself, at himself for having the voice, Ilan turns his thoughts back to their traverse of the Presidentials. They'd parked at the Mountain Club Hostel at the south end of the range. A Quebecoise New Hampshirite drove them around to the trailhead at the north end of the range where they took out their trekking poles, hoisted their packs and began hiking uphill. Yedit commented that it wasn't as bad as she expected. Not at all, Ilan agreed, just a winter day's hike. In fact, the thick pine forests covered in snow were darkly alpine, spoke more to lodges and hot chocolate spiked with peppermint schnapps than anything resembling high altitude adventure. In a matter of hours, they reached tree line. A sign at the end of the trail warned that many had died here, even in summer. Long feathers of rime ice streamed away from the back of the signpost, as if someone had collected a bundle of icicles from the eaves of a house and then glued them horizontally. Huge boulders fractured the snowfield. A rubble field! Yedit exclaimed. I love you, Ilan answered. She turned to him and he took her face in his gloved hand and kissed her cold lips. She blinked and teared up and bit her lower lip and sucked in her breath. He kissed her again and she bounced on her feet and suddenly blurted, thank you, thank you, thank you.

He pries her untouched coffee from her fingers and begins drinking it, glad that he convinced her long ago to give up sugar and milk. And what if her discomfort is simply that of performing an unsavory chore? They stare at each other and at the walls, silent, while Ilan's heart beats and beats and beats.

"You know, Yedit, I am serious about the *Shema*. There's that line that appears in the last psalm. And then there's the double implication that it declares not only that God exists, but heralds the Messiah's arrival. What about all the martyrs, all the people who died screaming it out?"

Three times, Yedit opens her mouth, like a fish trying to make air into water; three times, Yedit doesn't speak and each time Ilan asks her what, and each time she squints her eyes closed and shakes her head, no, and sucks in her upper lip and sniffles. Three times a day, Ilan remembers, he used to face east, take three steps backwards bow in three directions, take three steps forward, bow, and offer up his *Amidah* to God. In a sense, the destruction of the temple makes faith a far more individual practice. In the days of the temple, he would simply give tithing to the Cohanim and they would sacrifice animals on his behalf. He, perhaps, might say the *Shema*, and that would be that. But now words, the *Amidah*, stand in for animals. How about that for transubstantiation, Ilan thinks, speech into flesh. (Or was it flesh into speech?) Speech fails. His wife seemingly cannot speak. Cannot explain. And he cannot keep his own mouth shut. She did explain, the small voice whispers. That's not an explanation, Ilan replies.

"Well if it's not last night and it's not Louis and it's not that you want to see other people, then what the hell is it?"

"It's been for a long time now, Ilan. You know that."

"I don't understand."

"Stop pretending."

Fuck her, Ilan thinks. Fuck her. He'll screw his goddamn sales assistant. There's something about the freckles along the edge of her breast where her satin blouses' collars hang open. Or if not her, then there's Lorraine. He can't remember the last time he saw a twenty-two-year-old's ass naked. For a second he pictures the crease where her butt cheek will meet with her upper thigh; he tries to imagine her turning around to look at him while he screws her but instead he visualizes a conversion van full of cute local climbing chicks who pretend to study at SUNY New Paltz. But he can't lock in on any of their faces, can't distinguish between them. Instead, the word "cute" hovers in front of him as if it was a Zen kōan that he could masturbate to. He notices how Yedit's robe clings to the inside of her left breast, how he can see where her breastbone borders traces of rib. *That all of them are matimot: twin teeth, bicuspids, molars, or just twins, or just coupled.* He wonders if there is any way he can get her naked, be inside her body, a last time. *Your teeth, like a shorn flock that rises from the washing.* So would this be a last time then, he thinks, is this it? *That are all of them trimmed, and a childless one, one bereft of her young, there isn't amongst them.* And this is a metaphor for teeth that includes a pun on teeth, Ilan thinks. These are the flock of ewes come up from washing, their wool white, to which the lover's teeth are compared. None of them barren, all of them paired; paired how? With their mothers? Their lovers? Their brothers? Paired and the Hebrew is female and the image is easier when each ewe alone is bicuspid: round hips paired with round shoulders. Breasts. Two breasts of yours like two fawn.

Or did you want for your mother, Solomon? In all your thousand wives, had any a cunt so beautiful as the one that passed you? A vacuum opens before Ilan, vertigo pulls at his head and his stomach, at the coffee churning through his veins. He pictures a pastiche of bits of bars and body parts, a nebulous sexualized nightlife, himself and the Palestinian woman swirling on opposite sides of a whirlpool.

Which would he prefer, Bat Sheva or Yedit? One of the beautiful woman made from God's words alongside the universe during the six days of creation, who wedded Dovid and bore Shlomo, or the crazy Israeli woman he married sitting across the breakfast bar? The Louis voice in his head whispers: Yedit of course, because you're losing her. He wills her robe to fall open, the sash to untie, her body to expose itself. His life is about to end; he can feel that in his gut.

Dizziness. He should get to work, or get dressed, or call a climbing partner, or drink a bottle of vodka in a sitting, or go climbing, or call a friend. He reaches out and touches his wife's shoulder. She doesn't move his hand or her body away. Instead, she shakes her head once, violently, and sighs. But he leaves his hand in place—she doesn't want it there, she can take it off herself—and finishes her coffee, tipping the mug far back with his eyes open so that its interior momentarily seems a bottomless well, light ringing its periphery.

"I'm going to go pack a bag," Yedit says.

"Right, then."

"I think I need to be alone for that."

"But you aren't sure."

"Please."

Yedit stands up. Her lip trembles, but Ilan clenches his jaw. He lifts the mug up an inch, then sets it down loudly, pushes it into the other mug, envisions ceramic shattering on the terracotta flooring. She would lift her robe and jump back reflexively. Startled. Undone. But the struck mug only rocks back and forth, does not fall. She walks over to the refrigerator and opens its door. Ilan knows his refrigerator. The inside glows with soft white light diffused through glass shelving and carefully arranged bags of bright leafy greens, colorfully packaged containers of hummus, neatly labeled exotic cheeses. Ilan imagines her looking at the roast marinating for dinner. After a year of sobriety, they agreed he could begin cooking with wine again. Now, apparently, she doesn't care what he does.

He believes he can smell through her nose the rosemary, wine and beef. Perhaps he'll roast it even after she's left. Call Louis, who will bring over not his homemade rotgut, but a bottle of Cornas. One of Ilan's old favorites. A big thick French peasant wine.

Yedit likes what he cooks but he knows that the raw beef, the marinating ingredients, offend her. He suspects that she's looking for beer in the fridge. They've never kept beer in the house. A bottle of rum and one of gin so that she can have, and offer, the occasional cocktail. Some cheap wine for cooking. She shuts the door. Ilan imagines that she must be staring at her reflection in the steel door: a hazy and muddled mimesis.

"Have you spoken to your parents about this?"

"No. Not exactly."

"What did Joe say?"

"I haven't spoken to him about it exactly."

"Don't you think you ought to?"

"I'm going upstairs. Please. I'd like to be alone for a bit while I pack."

"They gave up everything to adopt you."

"Thank you, Ilan. That's plenty."

"To adopt an Israeli baby, orphaned by anti-Jewish aggression."

"I am not anti-Israeli."

"But you are anti-Jewish."

"I'm going upstairs."

"When the Romans flayed Rabbi Akiva alive for supporting the Bar Kochba rebellion, his dying words were the *Shema*. His students asked him how he could pray while he was being tortured to death and he said that he finally understood the meaning of God's gift of the prayer."

"He also said that everything he was, he was because of his wife."

"It wasn't her name he called out while he was being flayed!"

"And you really believe he had time both to say the prayer and explain to his students why he was saying it? The Talmud rabbis are liars."

Ilan remembers how Akiva's wife sent him away to learn Talmud for twelve years. When he came home, he overheard a conversation between his wife and a man criticizing Akiva's behavior. Akiva's wife said that she would have him learn for another twelve years. Overhearing this, Akiva snuck off before anyone knew he was home, and returned to his studies for another twelve years. But Jewish lore is full of men who don't visit their wives. Adam had to be commanded directly by God to return to Eve after the expulsion from Gan Eden. Uriah refused to visit Bat Sheva, which led King Dovid to have him killed. Would it have hurt Akiva to spend a night with his wife before returning to the Bait Midrash? Isn't there a commandment that a man must sexually satisfy his wife? I wonder, Ilan thinks, whether in that story I'm Akiva or his wife. The scholar or the scholar's support. Likely the latter. But, the small voice whispers, you're the one likely to die with the *Shema* on your lips. To be a martyr whose dying word declares God One. A frightening image of his house, abandoned by Yedit, comes to Ilan. In it, trays of acetone mixed with peroxide line the kitchen bar. Wire clippings and soldering tools litter the dining room. A sewing machine set up in Yedit's emptied office is surrounded by the materials for a vest lined with pockets filled with pennies.

Once, over dinner, in Pittsburgh, Ilan's father told him how Ilan's grandmother had been in a train accident. She and the man next to her were unharmed. Volunteers led them off of their derailed car and took them to a small field, sat them down, covered them with blankets, and ordered them not to stand up, no matter what. Ilan's grandmother told her son that from where they sat they could see that the car in front of them had flipped over, throwing people out of the windows. Screams for help came from inside of it. The man who'd been next to her said, We have to help. She'd replied that there were people helping; they were supposed to sit. I'm ok, the man said. I'm going to go help. "And then," Ilan's father said, "He stood up. And just like that," here Ilan's father clapped one hand on top of the other while making a whistling noise followed by an explosion noise, "He dropped dead, just dead, just like that. Shock. Shock killed him. No outside wounds but it killed him when he stood up and stressed his heart again."

Asshole, Ilan thinks, do you remotely believe that dumping you has caused Yedit such trauma that the exertion of leaving the room will kill her? No, he answers himself, It's myself I'm worried about. Nor, he continues, do you want her dead. But alive and happy without him? That also seems like a terrible outcome. And do you think staring at her leaning against the counter, on her feet ready to leave, will somehow reconcile you to this, he wonders. He starts silently repeating: if you love her then her happiness is more important than her being with you. And then the Sting lyric pops into his head: If you love somebody, set them free. Ilan hates fucking Sting.

He allows his eyes to lose focus until he can see the imprint of Anne's ass on the concrete countertop. But Yedit taps on the counter and forces him to recognize her. Ilan tries to see his wife, her pores, the lines around her mouth, how her hair hangs. He needs saving, not her, and yet he feels called upon to perform some act of heroism. For the first time, the Jewish laws that only allow the man to grant a *Get* make some real sense to him. Why, he wonders, is the entire middle of his marriage missing from his memory? He can easily recall their courtship, their early trips to New England and Quebec, their wedding, shopping for the house—not to mention his single life, the IDF, the killing. He can still mentally tour Anne's apartment, open every drawer and picture the contents perfectly —facial creams and peppermint sprays in the top right drawer of the dresser wedged into her doorless bedroom closet, accumulated while she temped at Aveda's headquarters—yes, he can do it. He can remember the wheat-pasted posters on the blue-painted plywood scaffolding over the Upper East Side store where they purchased napkins and placemats. In fact, he remembers the saleslady wearing a Tiffany bean necklace because Anne commented on it. He also remembers that he hated that Anne liked things like Tiffany bean necklaces. He sees Yedit again. But he can't recall how he and Yedit spent last week, what they had for dinner two nights ago. Obviously, last night, Louis dropped by with the jug of bad wine. That's all he can remember though. How is he supposed to figure out what's bothering Yedit if he can't remember anything? His vision blurs and he thinks, relieved, that perhaps now he'll begin crying.

"Diti, I don't want to forget."

Yedit groans gutturally, pushes herself up from the counter and walks out of the room. Presently, he hears her footsteps on the stairs. Each step creaks interminably beneath her weight. Halfway up, she stops, presumably on the sun-warmed patch of light again. Ilan drags his hands down his face pulling the skin away from his eyes. What to do? What to do? What to do? Should he go to work after all? Clearly they aren't going climbing. What a waste of a day off from the office: sitting home and watching, like an idiot, correction: as an idiot, while his wife packs her bags and leaves his house. The best thing to do in these situations is to continue on with one's normal routine, the things that have always given meaning to one's life. Remind oneself that that meaning persists in the face of disaster. He could call someone to go climbing. No. Maybe tomorrow, during the weekend. Only person available to climb on a Friday is Louis—well—To think, Ilan thinks, that I took a day off work so that my wife could leave me. And the sacrifice seems silly and simple. Why not just say the *Shema*? Declare God. Slit your wrists. Whatever.

It's unimaginable to do anything fun. But he should probably go into the office after all. Maybe he should call first. He really shouldn't follow her into the bedroom. She wants to be alone. She asked to be alone, demanded it. He shivers; all his clothing is up in the bedroom. He wishes he could transport himself to her parents' house in Nevada, sit down on the simple floral patterned love seat, the swamp cooler humming in the background, and drink a large glass of water. And how would that go? Ilan asks himself. There are so many simple ways to make powerful explosives: mix fertilizer with gasoline, blend acetone with car battery acid and hydrogen peroxide, order black powder by the keg for private loading of shot. Millions of ways to build something. Aesthetically, the black powder route holds the appeal of a long fuse leading to a sealed pipe. Aesthetically, little beats a belt lined with sticks of dynamite and a re-rigged ticking alarm clock. But clearly the best choice is a precipitate of triacetone triperoxide. Unstable, very explosive, fairly compact. Palestinian bomb-makers dubbed it Mother of Satan. It ain't sexy, but martyrdom isn't about showing off the fact that you could blow. It is blowing. And if his wife's leaving were a bomb, would it be for show? The sweating hostage-taker wrapped in rows of orange sticks crisscrossed with wire? Or would it be the simple raising of her arms to arm a trigger exploded by her arms' lowering?

If he went upstairs now, she'd be naked, or half-naked, or something in between. No, she'd be part-dressed, getting ready to leave. And for some reason, Ilan imagines her walking out of the house in a tan skirt suit leading Joe and Louis by the hand. Joe looking down at the ground and Louis turning to stick his tongue out. Ilan stands up. Don't be an asshole, he says out loud, but quietly, you don't have to let everything go. He turns the sink faucets on and off, admiring the way the porcelain extensions nestle in his hands. Then the same with the oven light; after that, the controller for the cooking lights, which are recessed under the over-counter cabinets. He walks out into the sunroom. He built the kick cabinets and covered them with cushions, found the Moroccan table, imagined the room. His own father never saw this house, but he came by Ilan's best city apartment. Twenty-seventh-floor two-bedroom two-bath with park views to the west.

Ilan sighs and puts his hand on a cold glass pane barely larger than the span of his fingers, hangs his head. So they'll sell the house. Stands to reason. At least he won't have to worry about re-caulking the peeling frames in front of him. He's barely gotten a chance to live in this house at all. Fifteen years from now, when the house has its two-hundredth anniversary, his and Yedit's brief tenure in it will hardly make a blip. Everything lasts longer than he can hold onto. Whoever moves here next will probably use the Viking range and steel-fronted refrigerator for decades. It will become theirs, and meanwhile, he'll never find anything like this again. He can't stay here without Yedit to share it with. (And who will she be with next? And will that man have a sufficiently long tenure—take true ownership of her—such that her marriage to Ilan becomes little more than a footnote in her life, a misstep, a steppingstone?)

For some reason he finds himself craving a Starbucks raspberry latte. More particularly, he wants to sit in the glassed extension of the Astor Place Starbucks staring down Lafayette Street, surrounded by NYU students and East Village hooligans. But the East Village doesn't exist in the same fashion that it did when he was twenty. And that Starbucks is no longer the same. There aren't long lines wrapping back from the dance studios across the street from the Public Theater, lines of respondents to the open-call auditions for Rent. Mightn't there be the same people, with the same aspirations, in line for some other musical? Ilan wouldn't know which show anymore. A decade later, they'd be different people anyway. No, I'd be a different person, Ilan realizes.

He walks into the living room, rubbing the goose bumps along his arms. Katja has been by to clean just Thursday, and everything is put away. When they first moved into the house, Yedit taught night class twice a week and he would get home and lay on the heap of furs and rugs and pillows in the alcove and read while he waited for her. She'd told him about a photographer for whom she'd worked as a personal assistant. The woman had a loft, mostly devoted to the chemical implementation of her craft. For a bedroom she'd hung a nomadic Yurt. Not one of the prefab deals Californians live in, but an actual Mongolian thing sewn from skins. This nook was their answer.

Ilan contemplates lying down on the furs now. As often as not, when Yedit came home from teaching, she would straddle him while he pretended to keep reading, distract him by pulling off her shirt and pinching her nipples. He would grunt and hold his book over his face while she began rocking her hips over his crotch. Sometimes she would lean over him and press her breasts into his face until he had no choice but to respond. Other times she would cavalierly get up and stalk out of the room. Force him to chase her. He feels the beginnings of an erection now and wonders if he can convince Yedit to make love to him a last time. "Asshole," he mutters. "Your wife is leaving you. Think about it."

After sex, after pinning her—or her pinning him—or some combination thereof—to whatever surface was at hand, he would be dispatched to the kitchen. Then Yedit would pull on her panties, pour herself a glass of sherry and sprawl on the furs with a copy of

Psalms or the *Song of Songs*. She would read softly to herself, marking the language's meter by gently tapping her brown anklebones against one another. If Ilan stood to the right of the stove, the angles between the breakfast bar's columns and the pass through to the living room allowed him to see a third of her at a time. He would slowly shift his stance to scan her body. The book in her hand, her elbows on the rug, a pillow between her triceps and the flats of her breasts propping her up. Her shoulders slightly higher than the base of her neck, rising above her black hair, suspended above the crushed sides of her breasts. And then the lean slope of her mid-body flaring in three dimensions into hips and ass so that even though they'd just fucked, even though he was hungry and cooking, he fantasized about tearing the crotch out of her panties, kneeling between those bent calves, clapping their perfect ankles, and shoving himself back into her.

He can hear her banging around upstairs. What a cliché, he thinks, to bang things around when you pack to leave your lover. What a cliché to imagine sex with a woman you can't have anymore as she prepares to leave. It would be effortless to take the four steps from the couch to the alcove, effortless to continue on through the glass windows into the yard. His penis flaccid, himself deflated, he looks down at his lower body. Swirls of hair cover a paunch that has the misfortune to grow more over his hips than his cock. I'm soft, he mouths. Do it now, break through the glass, the small voice encourages. Bloody yourself. It's difficult to move, though, to act. He's chilly, which makes him want to stand still. That weekend on the ridge below Mt. Washington it was so cold that when he woke up warm in his sleeping bag it seemed impossible even to cook breakfast. He would stare at Yedit, her face inches across the tent floor from his. She would wiggle around in her bag to bring a hand up to the drawstring-constricted opening around her cheeks and reach a few fingers to his lips. She would make breakfast, still in her sleeping bag, leaning out into the front vestibule to make snow into water, to bring water to boil for oatmeal. She transforms things,

Ilan mouths. The word 'translate,' as performed by his wife, takes on shiny metaphysical characteristics that he can't quite render into words. The things translated 'are.' 'Are' in the way Heidegger would describe a thing as having a "thingness." None of which makes much sense, Ilan notes, deflated again.

Himself, he stands still shivering. I could always blow up, he hopefully suggests. Not unless you purchase ingredients, counters the small voice, which requires leaving the house, requires setting up a laboratory and rendering explosives. It would require initiative and action, concludes the small voice. I've had those things, Ilan whimpers. He should have just said the *Shema* when that woman came up to his table at the café. Offered allegiance to his maker and then gone to meet Him.

Fast footsteps on the stairs confuse him. This is it. She's actually leaving. Should he hide in the closet or go back into the kitchen or meet her at the bottom of the stairs? He's naked; he's fucking cold; come on, man, move. Yedit reaches the first floor landing. He can hear her head towards the kitchen. She calls his name before coming into the living room. She stops with one arm on the doorframe and he follows her arm to her t-shirt's short sleeve and down from there to her pink panties. At least, he consoles himself, they aren't particularly sexy panties. But then, how much sexier must have been the woman in King Shlomo's song after the city guards beat her? She looks at him and opens her mouth. He can't feel an erection but worries he has one visible nonetheless. This is it, the humiliation of an adolescent's lack of control. Her mouth just hangs there, open. Finally she speaks.

"I was just wondering..."

"What is it, love?"

She bursts into tears. He walks to her, conscious of how he can see less of her as he gets closer, conscious of the way her panties fabric flutters loosely above the thin elastic binding it to her thigh. She lets him hold her, her arms limp by her sides. He smiles over her head, which is tucked beneath his chin.

Perhaps she would listen to his desire to translate the *Shema* if he pointed out the connection between Akiva and Rabbi Shimon. Shimon was Akiva's student, so of course there's that. More importantly, they both spent two twelve-year periods in exile. There are differences: Shimon spent his time naked in a cave, sustained by a carob tree while hiding from the Romans with his son. Growing up, the rabbis where Ilan learned at night during high school, and at the bait midrash in Tel Aviv where he studied on days off-duty during his army service, were fond of telling the story of Shimon's emergence from his cave. Notified by Elijah that the emperor Hadrian had died, Shimon and his son walked out into daylight. They came upon a man planting his crops and Shimon exclaimed, How can it be that this man does not spend all of his time learning Torah! And God smote the man, incinerated him where he stood. Father and son continued down the road towards the home from which they had been absent twelve years and came upon a man leading a donkey. This man as well does not devote himself to learning! Shimon exclaimed. This man too, God smote with fire. After the third such encounter, the third person besides each other that these two men had seen in twelve years—reduced to ash—God sent him back to his cave to learn for another twelve years.

What then, Ilan wonders, artificial lilac scent wafting from his wife's scalp, is the overlap between Akiva overhearing his wife and Shimon's being sent back by God? The overheard conversation could be construed as divine instruction. But Shimon wielded God and God spoke to Shimon. Shimon was correct about those people not learning, of course, or God would not have smitten them. But his time in the cave is always a punishment—first it is in lieu of death, and then to learn not to destroy God's world. Akiva's time at Yeshiva is a choice made possible by his wife's love (and his wife's money). Why hasn't Yedit told her followers to acknowledge Ilan as the source of their knowledge? He has enabled her financially and emotionally. Without his help she never would have finished the book, let alone published it. That too is a lie, Ilan thinks. I've only made things more comfortable. When Shimon and his son left the cave, they were covered in scabs from sitting naked in the sand. God sent them a carob tree, sustenance, Torah, but nothing more.

God is not in the business of making things easy, the small voice confirms; and Ilan glimpses a vision of himself desperate to get drunk, desperate to fuck the orange-haired colonel. Would greater strength have been the courage, the *koyakh*, to stay in Tel Aviv, marry Dalia, continue to practice Orthodox Judaism? Somehow, domestic life within the plush confines of Israeli modern orthodoxy doesn't seem exemplary of great fortitude. I needed to suffer, Ilan thinks. So this is your suffering? The small voice sneers, standing naked and fat in your expensive living room, holding your bitchy wife? Omelets just so? A big money job in a big money city? I climbed with Louis for years, Ilan counters, staring at a black and white photograph of Alaska's Chugach Range, hung over the couch. So what, the small voice replies, you got drunk, you got scared, you went someplace pretty. So what? You don't even do that anymore.

It's too much to muddle through and Yedit's face is warm against Ilan's chest. The Romans tortured Akiva to death. They ultimately honored Shimon for helping their princess. Ilan wonders whether those torturers ever longed for comfort. Yedit presses her arms against his chest. Slowly she steps back from his body and snorts, shakes her head.

Ilan looks at his wife, the famous translator. Her nipples poke against her blue top. He lifts her chin with his fist, concentrates on looking concerned, and kisses her. Her mouth tastes of salt and phlegm. He pulls her back towards him, holds her. She whispers that she meant to ask him if he knew where the suitcase with her winter clothing was. He murmurs her name over and over again, Yedit, Yedit, Yedit, rocking side to side, shifting his weight from one foot to the other, his legs spread, hers together and between his.

I'm not leaving, she whispers up at him and sniffles. He asks her why and she says that she can't—though they have so much work to do. He kisses her forehead and wonders aloud why they are both whispering. "Ok. Stay. I'm game for whatever you think we need to do."

The woman in his arms feels grimy. Can he possibly have compared her to Bat Sheva minutes ago? There's dirt on her shoulder and the lilac scent of her hair incompletely masks something vaguely unwashed. The composite other-woman he's contrived from parts of all the females he sees daily recedes behind a chain link fence guarded by Doberman pincers and machine gun towers, behind a swirling gray mist, a murk, a monochromatic era. He remembers the letter his father sent home several months after leaving that his mother did not show to him until he was eighteen. The letter had avowed that all the accoutrements of life—the house in Pittsburgh, his father's marriage, job, family—had all ultimately receded behind a single question, "But am I happy?"

Foreground that question, Ilan's father urged. Make better choices from the outset. Ilan swore that he would never ever use his father's fundamental question as a justification for any action or decision that affected those to whom he was committed. But that oath belonged to an era in which Dalia was his idealized partner. An era resplendent with faith in the Lord. An era in which shooting those who would kill Israelis was a mindlessly obvious affair. Now, he thinks, scanning his possessions, their possessions, over his wife's head: things, just all things, the kitchen, the knickknacks, the house, even the climbing, the cars and his job (Yedit?). Nonsense, static, a scrim between accurate decisions and his father's dreaded question. He crosses his arms and clasps her hands.

"If you're definitely going to stay, Yedit, then stay. I want you to. I want that. But if you're going to leave anyway, then leave now. Before there are things between us for which we can never forgive each other."

Her hands stop gripping his, though he holds onto hers. She looks away, looks back again. The sheen of her thick brown hair where it hangs over the curve of her olive cheekbones sends chills across Ilan's scalp. Her green eyes and lean, strong athletic body belong to an alternate universe that he has happened upon by chance. Punch your own weight, boy and this is not his own weight and here he is gambling it, doing so only because this strange and almost inevitably unsatisfying mélange of unknown woman nags at the back of his consciousness and because he can't tell whether the pink mottling across Yedit's cheeks is just tears or a lack of real attraction. You can be happy with someone less beautiful, if she loves you properly, he tells himself; and what constitutes properly, asshole? It feels like a freaking downgrade.

"Do you want me to stay or not, Ilan?"

"Do you want to?"

"Don't punish me."

"I need you to want to, really want to; for me to be able to do this, allow myself to be vulnerable, fight through the work ahead of us."

"I can understand that."

"We haven't done anything yet for which we need to hate each other forever. But if we don't handle this right, we will."

Her eyelids are puffy and pink. He thinks, I've done this; and he feels ashamed and he feels proud. She meets his eyes again. Everything about her is raw and right there in front of him. He can feel the hardwood floor give, barely, but give, beneath the balls of his feet and beneath his heels. He flexes his arches, lifting his toes. It is all he can do not to promise her he won't punish her. He spreads his arms, which, by a scissoring motion, cross her arms over her chest and pull her back into his body. With her hands in his hands folded behind her back, he kisses her and walks her backwards towards the wall. Her tongue, still salty, feels good against his, but her lips don't fit his mouth nearly so well as Anne's used to.

She frees her hands and pushes him away, wipes her mouth with the back of her wrist. His torso feels loose on his waist and he pants, lightly out of breath.

"No, Ilan. I was wrong. I do have to leave."

She slips sideways past him, her chest's not-contact palpable along his unclothed ribs. Then she's gone again, her footsteps again on the stairs, this time running.

"Your fucking winter clothing is in the crawl space above the bathroom toilet." He yells after her.

"Don't come up here."

"I won't."

Ilan looks around the living room for something to kill. And then he thinks, I actually want to hurt something. It feels good to feel violent, justifiably violent without qualification. Just then his research—and for the first time the word, 'research,' seems right—into homemade explosives seems like the timid first step of an exhilarating journey. Immolation, baby, yeah. And then his rage dissipates.

Who is she anyway? She's opaque. He can't imagine his way into her head at all. Doesn't even really want to right now.

In the hall closet, he finds a pair of orange Gore-Tex bibs that he hasn't worn since the ice-climbing season last winter and his red down jacket. Thus attired, he steps out onto the front patio. More flagstones. Which are cold beneath his feet. The sun, until then partially muted by the trees, finds its own now, blinding him. He coughs and sits down on the edge of a planter full of dying tomato vines, black-spotted green fruit withering between the rusting wires of their leaning cages. Go to work, he thinks, Work for the day. Meet some friends out afterwards. Don't drink. When you come home, she'll be gone. There is life after this. But he doubts it. There was Dalia. Then there was Anne. Then there was Yedit. Hope. Nihilism. Salvation. All of it is over now.

He coughs again. The elastic edge of the bib's right suspender rubs against his nipple. Wet frost-melt glistens along the tall grass stems. He twists his head around and sucks air between his teeth to avoid screaming. Alcohol, he thinks, bad homemade wine Louis brought over last night. A bungled attempt at a classic Chardonnay, or at least that's what the man who, for all Ilan knows, is fucking Ilan's wife said. (She isn't fucking Louis! Isn't she?) Maybe he could quit his job. He could work on the *Song of Songs* with Yedit. He'd translate the man's sections and she'd translate the woman's.

They'd write in two facing columns. It would be just like their early courtship, except now he'll also participate. This time, when the book gets published, they'll give call-and-response style readings in front of large public audiences.

Sure. Just like the couple employed by Hallmark to live in cabins on opposite shores of a Minnesota lake and write love poems back and forth. A fucking Punch and Judy show. Saccharine extra-deism. Love without God. An NPR gizz-fest. An anti-messiah of pink fleece and hot-chocolate with marshmallows. Fuck. If he could just accept God and accept death. If he could reach God, break through the membrane and really believe. Death.

He sucks in through his teeth again and swirls his head around. Coughs. Squints. On the far right edge of what would be termed lawn if they believed in mowing, a patch of winter squash looks close to ripe. Ilan stumbles to his feet and bumbles over. His nose starts to itch and he rubs his tongue against the roof of his mouth in an attempt to stop from sneezing. "Asshole," he says aloud. "Why did you drink the wine?

"Asshole, why did you shoot the Palestinian woman?

"Asshole, why don't you say the goddamn *Shema*? Just give in already. Weep and beg absolution."

And then he continues silently: Did you think you were going to prove something to Yedit by showing that you could do whatever this fucking bozo Louis did? Look at you now. The first sneeze comes and he convulses so hard that his ribs hurt. The Allegra is in the bathroom off the bedroom—yet another basic element of his life that he can not access, can not use to bring peace to his body—he sneezes again, his eyes squint shut, tongue spasms against the roof of his mouth, face flushes, sneezes again. God, he thinks, he'd shoot a thousand Palestinian women to feel comfortable in his own house, in the roof of his mouth. God: and it's not that there's no answer, but that silence is a wall. That's it, Ilan thinks, Judaism's holiest spot is a wall, an exterior wall, a mass of stone even the Romans couldn't quite bring down, behind which the *Shechinah* of God may somewhere still rest, behind which the golden dome of Islam's third holiest site rises. Paper prayers shoved in chinks. That's as good as it gets. The faded faces of 9/11-missing tacked to plywood barriers and left to fade in the elements. From dust to dust; so goes man's beseeching screams, his desperate need for deity. More, Ilan wants more.

How do you ask God for more?

If the paper prayers don't work?

If killing his enemies haunts you?

You corrupt his work. Reinterpret the psalms, the *Song of Songs*, the *Shema*, *Samuel*, the five books of Moses. Become Yedit and if that's not an option, align yourself with her. Dare God. But Ilan needs more.

How do you ask the woman upstairs packing a bag for more?

If she's stronger than you now?

If she neither needs nor wants you?

If you can't make her listen to memories of winter camping trips and afternoons under the cherry trees? Ilan would shoot a thousand Palestinian women to have never shot one. You could have said the *Shema*, finished your espresso, and left for heaven, the small voice condemns. But you are not strong.

Maybe he should just go up to the bathroom. He can tell her about his plan for the *Song of Songs*. But then, maybe the plan has a better chance if he waits for her to come downstairs and outside, then at least she'll see that he respected her wishes. Respect vs. medication. Maybe if he translated a small section first and started with that—though what if he starts sneezing while he's trying to recite it? Surely she can't get mad if he comes into the bathroom to get his medication. Yedit knows how badly his allergies affect him. Don't be sure of anything, asshole, he cautions himself, fighting back a sneeze.

They should have pushed on to the summit of Mt. Washington, he thinks. They could have made it to the top. Yes, there had been a whiteout. But there was trail enough to follow. It wasn't as if they were in danger of stepping off a cliff. They'd been so close to the summit. A mile, maybe, of trail, a few hundred vertical feet. It wasn't as if they hadn't had a tent and sleeping bags. Worst came to worst, they could have simply dug in and waited out the storm. Instead, he had told her that it was more honorable to descend under their own power without summiting than to top out, only to have to beg help from the weather station up there.

She supports him in his recovery from those weaknesses he can't escape: jitteriness around loud noises, an inability to turn down subsequent drinks. In turn, he's unflappable on vertical ascents. But she's caught up with him. Is as strong a climber as him. Understands that he is afraid, that he can't objectively assess real hazard when they back off routes or climbs or summits. Maybe if they topped out on Mt. Washington, he wouldn't be walking around the yard, sneezing, while she packed clothes for seasons ahead.

Ilan reaches the patch of vines. Dandelions gone to seed sprout along the raised rows, them and strange sage-colored weeds with leaves like cubist paintings, each myriad angle ending in a razor thorn. Yedit asked him to weed weeks ago but the climbing has been too good and they haven't spent any time in the garden. He sneezes again. Snot races from his sinuses. With a thumb against his right nostril, he farmer blows; then does the same with the other side, long ribbons of clear mucus stream out from his nose. Fuck. Since her book published she hasn't exactly been a wiz for chores either. He wipes the snot off with the back of his hand and then wipes that against the Cordura-reinforced seat of his bibs. Well the squash is growing fine, weeds or no weeds. He turns on his heels; wonders how long he will have to wait before he can go up to the master bedroom's small bathroom and take his allergy medicine. So Yedit is packing her stuff. She'll leave and not tell him where she was going. She'll simply get in her car and drive away. Anne's number is probably still in his desk at the office. His stomach bothers him but he doesn't want to go into the house, not even to take a shit.

Going inside to get to the upstairs bathroom, though, that he would do. Get his allergy medicine out of the cabinet they found in an antique store off Route 2 a hair north of Williamstown. Its border of painted wildflowers faded rather than wilted; discolorations blossom behind the glass, mottle the faces it reflects. During their first year of marriage, with all the extra time created by not dating and not drinking, they'd begun an obsession of three-day, weekend climbing trips, often extending their way to take Yedit through parts of New England she'd never visited. Well what was she going to do, take the cabinet off the wall and bring it with her? It would go with the house and no one would give a shit about it. A family would probably move in here, one that didn't cook, no doubt, or didn't cook in a way that began to justify the kitchen renovations, the convection ovens and strategically situated workstations for chopping and washing, the extra burners on the kitchen island for sautéing away from the main cooking area. And though a new kitchen adds value to a property, it doesn't add value in kind. No, basically he'd built the fantasy showroom for his cooking dreams that he would not get to exploit. The new family would probably show up, and, if they had income to buy a place like this and lifestyle to buy a place like this, both parents would probably need to work to keep the kids in appropriate schools and practices and activities. They'd eat frozen food and TV dinners and quick recipes gleaned from websites. Their children would trample mud through the immaculate, sparely decorated corners that he and Yedit had created, subsuming and consuming the ghosts of the children that he and she would never have, not now. Who is she, anyway, he silently demands of the withered grass, to take all these things away from him?

This new family seems to be peaking out the windows at him. They'd hang curtains where Ilan and Yedit had embraced the watchful voyeurism of the woods. They'd invite friends over and show off the amenities they didn't use. Ilan remembers so well the long walk home from his first job on Water Street. He'd turn off Water onto Nassau, eye the glitzy suits in shop windows, their pant cuffs always, inexplicably, knotted. Now he knows that those are cheap suits, chintzy material. Then he had been enamored of their low prices, though those prices, too, had been beyond his reach. Where Nassau gave way to Lafayette, the porthole-pocked green tiles of the municipal jail divided City Hall's outliers from Chinatown. Where Lafayette crossed Canal, street vendors peddled lo mein for a dollar a box next to stacked cartons of greens that Ilan, in his middle age, finally knows the names for: bok choy, Napa cabbage, Chinese broccoli, daikon. As often as not, he'd pick up dinner, eat while he walked past the old white stone police station converted into condos, the nineteenth-century French-style townhouses across from the Public Theater, Astor Place. Development where Lafayette becomes Fourth Avenue and where Fourth Avenue crosses Fourteenth Street has so completely removed whatever was there that Ilan can't even recall the original scenery of his decade-and-a-half-old walk.

Seedy, it was seedy, he thinks.

Past Fourteenth, Fourth became Park Avenue. North of Union Square, the Nineteenth Century's hyper-adorned grandeur yielded to ever-taller buildings. Windows upon windows of velvet curtains, furniture spun of Milanese glass, walnut-handled Barcelonan briefcases, Tsarist tea services, customs shirts and custom shoes and custom stereos, trappings of a life Ilan briefly inhabited after his trading business took off and before he met Yedit and sobered up.

I live in this farmhouse now, he thinks. I live here. The new family never started a career without a college degree, without money. Their mentors never told them that it was more important to dress like you went to Harvard than to have gone to Harvard.

They've changed Union Square and now they're going to take away my house, he despairs. On Fridays, he would pick a dive bar in the East Village for happy hour. If he met a woman he would stay. More often, he continued to the apartment on eighty-fifth and York that he shared with three strangers, or to the two-dollar Cineplex Odeon on Fiftieth Street. That's gone too, he mouths. Money, everything's money now. Ilan has money. But they'll take away your house, the small voice assures him.

He walks through the side yard to the shed at the far edge of the rear patio. When God gave Avraham the Promised Land (promised him the Promised Land), Avraham set out to walk its boundaries, and from that, the commentators tell us, we learn that one way to mark possession of real property is to walk its borders. Yes, Ilan thinks, I'm retaking possession of my property. From the second shelf inside the sienna shed Yedit insisted he build rather than buy an "ugly" Rubbermaid thing, Ilan pulls a weeding fork and spade, matched by their heavy green plastic handles whose pebbled grips are mortared with dirt from happier summers. Mt. Washington and three-day climbing weekends weren't Yedit's only escapes. When she was too nervous to sit still, she would come out into the backyard. She would, Ilan thinks, pretend to be an American woman. No one, he chuckles, ever made a worse mess of flowerbeds. Perhaps, he continues, I shouldn't have had Anne here that afternoon. Perhaps I shouldn't have slept with her.

There was a dream. A dream of walking into ABC Carpet and Home and purchasing giant pieces of antique teak. A dream of sophistication. Of class. I'm wearing orange plastic pants and a red winter coat while my wife packs enough of her belongings to ditch our middle-class dream house, Ilan thinks.

We never made it, he thinks.

He stands for a moment, a tool in each hand, blinking. Last year, this time of fall, they'd flown to Israel and missed a healthy chunk of the climbing season. Yedit's translation of *Psalms* came out, and, bizarrely, (how often, Ilan thinks, do I attach the word bizarre to my wife's successes?) a Tel Aviv bookstore elected to promote it heavily. Her parents flew with them to see their daughter read internationally. Several local editors took them out to dinner their first night in town, to a French restaurant that would have blended in effortlessly in the East Village. One of the editors, who looked the way Ilan, as a boy, imagined all Israelis looked—European and cosmopolitan and spy-like: black hair graying around the temples, strong understated physique, dark rather than tan, green eyes, salt-and-pepper chest hair showing where his dress shirt's collar opened—joked with

Yedit that now that she had created a translation of a piece of the bible that only atheists would read, they should really translate her version back into Hebrew so as to reach a wider audience. "Just the sort of thing that we're talking about for these settlers, yes?"

"Modern Hebrew is a different language than Biblical Hebrew is a different language than English. And they don't translate. What I've done is, truly, to re-envision the story. You want me to do that again into Hebrew so that the Shasniks can really hate you, I'll do it."

Ilan and his in-laws gradually retreated from the other diners' consciousness, a consciousness that orbited Yedit. Ilan mentioned to his father-in-law, Joe, that for a while after the army he'd taken painting very seriously. Joe said that he was so very proud of his daughter, an academic being treated like an artist, like a rock star. When she was little, Joe confided, he would warm milk for her before bed, and she would sit sipping it and playing with his cuticles for hours, daydreaming, not going to bed.

Ilan sighed. "We might as well not even be here."

"We're not here for Yedit, Ilan; she's here for us, for us to watch, to get *nachas*."

"Is this *nachas*? joy? Is this where it ends? Her parents die fighting Arabs and this is the end result?"

"We're her parents," Joe said.

"She renounces God, makes a living of it."

"She's a poet."

"Without God, what the hell are we doing here?"

"She doesn't care about these men; stop being jealous," said Yedit's mother.

"Jealous? They're lost in her. They've forgotten we're here. What good would jealousy be?"

"So you're not jealous of the attention she's getting?"

"My issue is what good is being Jewish? Why not just give up the game and join the goyim?"

"How can you say that, Ilan? Her parents died fighting the Arabs." Joe said. "You're an Israeli, a hero even."

"For what? For what? Without God who gives a shit about this? That we're Jews? To kill people?"

Ilan took a sip from his glass of water. Everyone else drank wine. The group of male editors surrounding Yedit seemed to actively drift from the table, as if a spotlighted section of floor rapidly moved further away from Ilan and his in-laws. Ilan knew that Susan and Joe were the wrong audience. Not simply because they loved their adopted Yedit, but because they weren't intellectuals. Does being an intellectual simply translate into being fucked up about questions of existence? By what standard is Ilan an intellectual? Training? Education? Scholastic production? Of course not. You're an intellectual, the small voice says with the rising lilt of a Rabbi unveiling an epiphany, because you're the sort of Jew too weak to fight against those who would kill you. You're the sort of Jew who would let a holocaust happen rather than lift arms, shed blood.

Even after Ilan's father left him, left Pittsburgh, sacrificed all moral high ground, on those rare occasions that he broke bread and drank wine with his son he took great pleasure in pointing out that, "Whenever the Jews forget that they are Jews, God sends someone to pin a gold star on their chest. Reward for their efforts."

Tamed by the futility of his attack, Ilan, supplicant, asked his in-laws, "Why do you persist in supporting Israel, in calling yourselves Jews?"

They looked at him. He didn't need them to say that only a Jew could come up with a question like that.

Ilan sighs and sits down in the middle of the vines, crushing some of them a bit. He stares at the two tools in his hands. He lifts the weeding fork and mutters: *The voice of my lover! Behold-it approaches.* Lifts the spade and mimes its reply: *Rise to me, my love, my beauty, ulechi-lakh*[11]. They could have, they could have, they could have! Have what? Sat across the kitchen counter reciting the *Song of Songs* to each other? Moved to Minnesota like the Hallmark-writing-couple? Ilan trades abstractions—commodities, stocks, paper, options—in a wood-paneled suite downtown. *Ulechi-lakh: and go.* The objects in his hands are not biblical puppets, they are clumsy apparatus with which he could have avoided irritating his wife months ago by doing what he's going to do now: weed.

Couldn't they translate sections of the *Song of Songs* to each other over the mill pond up at Minnewaska? *And go with me, go away, go away with me, because look at the water: it passes over us.*

No gardening gloves—well the hell with gardening gloves. When he stands up to turn around, blood rushes from his head and he feels so dizzy that for a moment he thinks he might fall over. With his hands on a berm, he lowers himself back down onto his knees. A robust, thorned weed grows directly in front of his face. Without gardening gloves, it will be impossible to pull. He wonders how best to attack this new nemesis. Anne would have loved having a garden, but the whole time they dated, they both lived in apartments, high in buildings surrounded by concrete sidewalks that bordered asphalt bound by even more cement. Now that he finally lives in a regular house with a regular yard and his clothes are all locked away with yet another woman leaving.

Even the botanical gardens had originally been introduced to him by Anne. He met the director at an evening picnic for members to which he'd been Anne's date, and there they began discussing short-term trading strategies. True, he hadn't much cared for going to the gardens with Anne. But then, lots has changed about him since then.

A great sob expands in his lungs but he suppresses it, exhaling forcefully instead.

All he wants, he knows, is to go to the cherry orchard and lie in the sun and just not worry about anything for one, goddamn afternoon.

The rising sun makes him uncomfortably warm in the down jacket. He takes it off and immediately feels chilly. A new series of sneezes rises in his head. Eyes watering, he desperately rubs his tongue against the roof of his mouth. Miraculously, the sneeze-need subsides. Well, if he can't pull this ugly, thorned weed, he decides, then he'll dig it out. The ground is hard and his little spade rasps like a gravedigger's shovel, hardly moves any earth at all. He takes another swipe. Deeper this time, more effective. Good. Several inches below the surface, he discovers, to his surprise, looser soil. Ilan shoves the spade's blade in to its hilt, and, using both hands, twists out a decent quantity. In the attic, he has all of his painting supplies left over from college and several fitful starts thereafter.

Now that he's sober, and soon to be single, perhaps it will be a good time to give climbing a rest, begin painting again. What he means to say is that he might channel any pain caused by this breakup into art, or something like that. Yes, he tells himself, the Times article will read: Recovering addict turns pain into art. The reviewer won't be particularly jazzed about his art per se, but will discuss him, in absentia, as being a savant (though not as talented as a real savant) who manages to live simply by the power of art. The abstraction of art as healing force: powerful. His art: not very interesting. In the article's photo, he'll have badly-coiffed gray hair and thick glasses and wear paint-splattered white overalls that protrude over his belly and the article will whisper, shocked: this man used to be a stock broker. Stupid. To even imagine himself suddenly transformed, hanging out at a gallery explaining his work to patrons at an opening, to art reporters. What a dumb idea. Why can't he just do something for himself without the goal of public success? Besides, the whole image suggests that he's letting his wife leave so that he won't have to climb anymore. First he used the excuse of his marriage to get out of climbing dangerous routes with Louis. Now that his wife's strong enough to climb routes that scare Ilan, he's getting out of the marriage. When did I become such a fucking coward? Ilan wonders. The hole grows bigger. Soon, it will make sense to angle in towards the roots of the large plant. As things stand now, it looks like he plans to plant a second large thistle. Yes, that's it: the weed is a thistle.

A door slams somewhere inside the house. A moth settles onto the green, prickly bulb at the terminus of one of the weed's branches. Ilan stops digging and watches its white and brown wings spread open, join vertically, then rest ninety degrees apart, each forty-five degree above horizontal. Its tiny cocked feet cling to the barely emerging purple tassels of the about-to-bloom thistle bud. Somehow, the bug reminds him of navy recruitment commercials. Fighter jets on aircraft carrier decks at dusk. Oily black skies traced by deck lights and flight signals, inflamed by a setting fireball, wings twisted up in sharp angles. Only, asshole, you decided to go back home to Israel, he mutters to the bug, you decided to go defend your true homeland.

Neither his Hebrew nor his eyesight were sufficiently strong to win the privilege of killing aerially; Ilan saw his victim, saw her lips twist as she collapsed. Ilan was close enough to the woman he shot to hear the sound her body made against the pavement.

Ilan left Anne three times before she left him, and when she left, when she stood from her seat, rose from the prix-fixe dinner they were eating at one of the two outside tables of a small restaurant in Antibes, and walked back to their hotel room, there had been a period of about thirty minutes, during which he finished their bottle of wine, in which he'd been genuinely relieved that she was finally ending things. Her and not him. He hadn't slept at all during the two days it took to get on a flight back to New York. He went to their couples' counselor first thing after landing and she told him, as he sat there, shaking, cowed by sleep deprivation, that sometimes people simply needed to move on with their lives, enter new phases and, for better or worse, they couldn't always take their lovers with them. He should really just let Yedit go. Shake hands, hug maybe, smile, laugh, cry, cherish, *recuperate for good*, the years they'd spent together.

Eight inches down into his now foot-wide hole, Ilan strikes a layer of soil choked with rocks that leaves long white marks on the spade's blade as it scrapes between them. Let her go, he counsels himself. Let Yedit go. Clearly, she needs this. Perhaps you need it too. You never know. After some time goes by, and she has a chance to think about things, she might even come back. Anything is possible. Ilan inhales through his nose as deeply and slowly as he possibly can. The air he forces into his lungs feels warm and dirty, barbed almost.

Be cool, man. Be cool.

He reverses his grip on the spade, holds it two-handed over his head, and then strikes down into the soil with all of his force, plowing the dirt out between his legs steam shovel style.

And again and again and again.

The hole grows dramatically, though it doesn't seem to affect his razor-thorn-sporting nemesis at all. Sweat runs from his hair and stings his eyes. He can't stop to wipe them: his arms are covered in dirt, which, mixed with perspiration, has already become damp and muddy. Wiping them across his eyes would just make the stinging worse. He can't tell whether it would be better to cry or not cry. He can't tell whether he should run upstairs, sit on his wife's bag, and explain to her how when he realized that theirs was a morning relationship, that after they kissed under the cherry trees, he'd torn all the pages out of his address book, destroyed the means of contacting the various women he'd hung out with in various capacities in the years after (and before) Anne had left. He will run upstairs and explain to her that he can't live without the giddy seriousness that comes over her face when she approaches a climb, or without the way her hands feel on his back when she soothes him to sleep, or without the awkward clumsiness with which she's breaking her way through their third set of dishes since they got married, or without the goofy grin and little girl's voice she uses to tell stories about her day's teaching. He will tell her how proud he is of her accomplishments: her book, her tenure, her interviews with the New York Review of Books and All Things Considered. He will tell her how she's saved his life, made him healthy again—he might not be able to stay sober without her, not be able to keep working and climbing and sane and productive and happy. He keeps digging, tearing up roots, possibly those of the thorned nemesis, but as likely as not, more likely he tears at the roots of those of the vines he is supposed to protect. She hasn't saved his life anyway—it's sobriety that's saved his life, really. He should respect her wishes: if she wants to leave, she should leave; people are allowed to leave.

He looks at his pit. Foxhole. He is digging a foxhole. An entrenching tool would help. From his position, he can cover the front entrance of the house and the driveway. Yedit will call the police if he forces her back into the house by firing from a foxhole in the melon patch. They'll storm the driveway behind riot shields, lob grenades from low-flying helicopters. Headlines will read: Survivor, Israeli hero, former soldier cracks, barricades wife in house, holds off police for hours.

The sun creeps over the trees.

Ilan shields his face with a dirt-crusted hand. Facing east while covering his morning eyes elicits *Shema Yisraeil Adonai Eloheinu Adonai Echad.* He stops himself there by reminding himself that he doesn't believe in that crap anymore. But the *Shema*'s declaration that there is only one God predates all other Jewish prayer, and, likewise, resists his attempts to dislodge it from his brain. Disgusted, Ilan demands to know whether he isn't next going to whisper, *Baruch sheim kivod malkhuto l'olam va'ed.* Or even, for that matter, continue on with the prayer's next three paragraphs. Fuck it. But then, doesn't the question itself contain the whispering of that second line?

The truth is that Ilan doesn't have access to prayer. The truth is that Yedit could simply leave through the back door out to the patio, slip off into the woods, and disappear. The truth is that he no longer owns a firearm, hasn't for many years, in fact. The truth is that he doesn't want to fire upon anyone, or trap anyone, or hold them in the house. He wants to not want those things, wants to let Yedit simply walk out of the house. And, he wonders, am I simply keeping my cool because I think she might come back? And if I stop believing she'll change her mind, is there something I should be doing now? Something stronger? The foxhole, if it ever really reaches those dimensions, is meant for hiding from himself, not armed defense.

I'm a scaredy-cat, deflated, a bag of a man, Ilan thinks. Just last week, when Ilan realized that he had gotten as far as placing an order for enough ingredients to clothe a platoon in TATP-charged vests, he ran down the hallway from his office to the men's room, noting the SVP-of-sale's tan alligator-skin loafers below the stalls' dividers, before shoving his pants down, barely in time before his bowels broke, no time to put down a seat liner. Fucking SVP over there, he thought, who needs that shit? Another explosive wave wracked his lower body as the shoes left the next-over stall and made their way to the sinks. How long is that fucker going to wash his hands? Eyes closed, Ilan inhaled slowly through his nose. His heart rate didn't so much accelerate or pound, but flutter, uncontrollably, like a flailing hummingbird. He began to exhale and then spun around, any ambiguity about his stomach's resilience decided by his shit's stench, and threw up into the toilet, legs spread wide and head suspended, the motion sensor automatically flushing the bowl, a few particularly violent drops spraying up onto his bracing hands that gripped the seat sides. So that's where those little water drops come from, he thought, feeling better about having put his ass directly on the seat. He'd always figured the spots were piss.

"Hey are you ok in there?"

"I'm ok."

"You sure?"

"Shouldn't have eaten at Subway."

Ilan left the stall and the SVP was waiting for him, shaking his head. With a wet stack of paper towels, he began dabbing at Ilan's face. Ilan didn't feel stable enough to resist. The SVP patted Ilan's shoulder and told him to go home early. Ilan wondered at the calm of this man who had color in his skin, a smile on his face, warmth in his hands. The man was a miracle. Ilan thanked him—though without any intention of leaving work early.

"Get some rest, ok?"

Ilan submissively agreed to.

But really, he insists to himself, give me a gun and I could keep her from leaving the house.

A building itch behind his sinuses returns Ilan from fantasies of death by police gunfire. He sits, cross-legged, shirtless, orangebibbed, on the edge of his hole and frantically rubs his tongue against the roof of his mouth. Sweat runs down his forehead, around the sides of his nose and stings his eyes, he raises the back of his wrist as high as his nose before remembering that it is covered in dirt. The gig is up. The first sneeze convulses his body. His stomach contracts, his chest tightens, his neck tenses. He sneezes again and his legs fly out into the hole. More doors slam inside the house. He sneezes again, and again, in rapid succession now. Tears completely overfill his eyes. A fly buzzes around his left ear and he blindly swats at it. Mucus runs from his nose in long strands and he opens his mouth, *gahhing* and gasping, in a weird involuntary attempt to get his chin out of the way. He leans over his pit and attempts a farmer-blow but the run simply sticks to his hand in long sticky strands. Shaking his hands sends zygotes of dirt-inseminated clear snot flying into his pit and onto his legs and chest. Rubbing his hands on the dirt muddies them worse than they were, but makes them, at least, less sticky, less gross, somehow. He gasps for breath. A new round of sneezes seems ready to burst through his sinuses. He brings both his fists down on either side of him, as hard as he can and screams: "Fucking bitch!"

The front door opens and Yedit steps out. She shoulders the red Gregory pack with yellow rip-stop gridlines that Ilan bought her for their trip to Mt. Washington. Tears continue down her face, messing the black mascara with which she's ringed her eyes. But when she sees Ilan sitting at the edge of his pit, and when a bubble of snot forms around his nose, she starts laughing, laughing in a kind way. Ilan mumbles: "Fucking bitch." But his heart isn't in it. She walks up to him, her head to one side, laughing, sniffling. His shoulders slump. He can feel the slump like a full note on the bass end of a piano keyboard. He tilts his head back to look at her. She stands over him, lets the fingers of her left hand drift down to his forehead.

"I love you, Yedit."

"You're a lovely man, Ilan."

"I don't want you to go."

"I'm sorry."

"Can I call you?"

"I'll call you."

"And what about the work I've done for you?"

"Work?"

"On *Shir haShirim.*"

Her fingers drift away from his forehead, barely brushing the edge of his hair as they take off, as she makes a sound both guttural and nasal. He twists around to look at her back. Don't, he urges himself, Don't go after her. Let her go. Don't. She heads for her Rav 4, a silly car that she purchased, used, from a student despite Ilan's offer to put her in something sexy. Her ass, jeans-clad, pressed down by the pack's waist-belt, sways and swoons in his vision. Leave her go. God, but her body. Then she calls back behind her that Ilan should, if possible, try not to destroy the garden entirely, though if what makes him happy is dressing up in plastic overalls and digging a hole to China, that's understandable too.

He's up, standing, swaying, spade and gardening fork held out in front of him. He walks towards her: "You can't go."

"I need to."

"I need you."

"Please stop."

"You don't understand. I need you."

"I heard you the first time."

"But I need you."

Yedit ducks into her car and slams the door. Ilan runs towards the mini-truck. She hits the electric locks and starts the engine. He slaps the hood and throws up his hands as she backs out. He yells for her to wait and she slows.

"Do you mind if I drink with Louis tonight?" He asks, walking alongside her door, gravel crunching uncomfortably beneath his bare feet.

"Ugh. Why would you do that?"

"I wish I could be strong and just let you go, move on. But I'm not; you know I'm not."

"I can't discuss this right now. I'll call you."

She puts the car back into gear and begins backing up. Ilan yells for her to stop, real panic in his voice. "Stop!" he screams.

"Fuck you!"

She gives him the finger and accelerates into Louis' Jetta behind her. The impact throws her head backwards into the headrest. Louis' horn blasts and her head ricochets into the windshield, fracturing it. Instantly, the glass turns opaque. Ilan can see nothing more of truck's interior. He can feel the weight of a gun in his hands and he thinks: did I kill her? The thought awes him. She was about to detonate and he killed her. He approaches the stopped vehicles carefully, one leg cautiously crossed in front of the other.

The *monodrone* of Louis' horn ceases.

It's just her then. A crow cries through the new silence, and Ilan hears, with startling clarity, the individual stones grinding beneath his feet. I can call Anne, now, he thinks. Anne will forgive my calling if I tell her Yedit's dead.

Louis' car door opens as Ilan reaches the left corner of the jeep. Ilan throws a hand up in air; Louis, still sufficiently programmed a soldier, halts where he is. There's blood, not a lot, but blood, at Louis' hairline and he's tender with his right arm, rubbing its shoulder with his left hand.

This is it, then, Ilan: You're life began by killing a stranger with whom you have since fallen in love, and then ends with the death of a lover you've quite nearly estranged.

But is it, then? And why is Louis here anyway? Louis who has stopped rubbing his shoulder and stares straight at Ilan. Ilan blinks his eyes hard to clear his head—he dare not shake his head now, lest shaking signal.

Yedit is the Palestinian woman is Yedit.

This is the sidewalk in Tel Aviv. She went to leave, he distracted her, and she died. Her body is a bomb. Really? Come on.

"Yedit is the Palestinian woman," he says aloud.

Louis, apparently freed by Ilan's voice, approaches.

Louis speaks, but Ilan refuses to hear him. Ilan refuses to hear the cursing from inside the mini-SUV. Instead, he places a hand on the door-handle. He girds himself, grits his teeth, reiterates the absolute necessity of treating his wife's body with the same caution that he treated the suicide bomber's body.

"God takes away everything," Ilan mutters.

"Maybe take a minute," Louis says.

Before Ilan can pull the door open, Yedit pushes it open and steps out, swatting at the now deflated airbag. The door between them, Ilan scans her for blood, ready for sudden pools of black. He reaches over the door towards her to check her pulse, but she's out of reach. A mix of acrid and sweet smells, gas and explosives. He pushes the door with his body to get towards her and grabs her shoulders but she pushes him away. She turns towards Louis, towards decimation.

"Is your car all right?" Yedit asks.

"You're ok, Ilan," Louis says. "Everything is ok."

"Would you move your fucking car then, Louis?" she asks. "Please? Now?"

Ilan tells Louis not to do it, his wife is hurt, they should attend to her first before dealing with vehicles, there's shock to consider. Yedit tells him to shut up. She's fine. It's just the airbag went off, which it isn't supposed to. Louis tells Ilan not to move, not to worry, he's just going to move the car and be right back. And Ilan remembers to breathe, breathes and visualizes himself, dirt and snot covering his face and arms, eyes red from allergies and tears, orange-bib clad, barefoot, breathes, visualizes, and deflates. The windshield isn't even cracked. The collision, at worst, bent the bumpers. Ilan gestures to them to go ahead. Yedit inhales in a way that lifts her shoulders and chest and head, and then exhales audibly through pursed lips. He's just moving the car, Louis promises. Yedit quietly thanks Louis and Louis gingerly walks backwards to the Jetta. Louis and Ilan still have eye contact. Louis gets back into the Jetta, motioning again to Ilan to stay put.

Yedit climbs back into her truck, the white bag draping her lap like a surgeon's smock.

Ilan takes a step back as first Louis and then Yedit start their cars.

He waves, or tries to wave, as they back up.

He waits for a second sound of impact that doesn't come.

Part 3:

Same Day/Altogether Different

Ilan pulls his pillow over his face, shielding his eyes from the sunlight eating at their still-shut lids. Trace scents of his cologne mix with Anne's perfume and his shampoo and the slightest underbelly of something unwashed, almost lye-like, reminiscent of national park chemical toilets and the profoundly retarded men he cared for one summer during high school. He sits up and flings the pillow away. It hits something on the dresser that falls, cracks, and rolls. Ilan curses and opens his eyes. Booze vapors. He thinks proudly, this is the first morning he's woken up to something other than *the creations of his hands speak the firmament*[12], or wondering why a God who would destroy his hounded people's enemies would allow those enemies to rise against his people in the first place, or thinking about how he could have saved the Palestinian woman, forced her hands to her sides and away from the bomb's trigger, forced her to feel his breath, her dissipating, her heartbeat muffled by the explosives between their clothing. His abdominal muscles tremble at what he might have done, probably did do, last night. So you were an asshole, he whispers, and crawls to the foot of his bed. In the silent spaces between his sheets' rustling, tinnitus suggests footsteps approaching from the foyer: Anne, boss, police. Then the spaces suggest the lost woman, the failed terrorist. Asshole, why did you think about not thinking about it? That ruins everything. And then he reminds himself, not as if you've never felt this before. Always ends up ok. A bottle of Laphroig lies on the floor, neck cracked, oozing. And then, sure: ok, if survival is enough.

In the master bathroom, he takes a box of Alka Seltzer Morning After down from the already-opened medicine cabinet. Stretches, box held over his head. Brings his arms down against his muscles' desires. Last packet. Wishes, not for the first time, that he could escape his body. He crumples the box and throws it next to the toilet. Then whispers: *odicha, al ki nora'ot niphleti*[13]. No, fuck escaping the body; he can keep the body; it's thinking that's traumatic. So much for believing he'd woken up without Yedit Manus' book in his head. *Nora'ot: fearfully, inspiring fear, awesome. Niphleti: I am miraculous.* No, hopeless and wonderful. Ilan looks down at the box on floor, the trash on the floor, litter in his bathroom. He can't summon guilt, can't summon shame. Not just because Sonya raised her rates but because, because who knows. *Miraculous are your creations, and my soul knows a lot.* No, nothing. Ilan can't make himself feel just now. He shuts the medicine cabinet and his bicep appears in its mirrored door. He flexes, then relaxes, evaluates himself: skin a bit too pasty, too flesh-like, nose a bit swollen again, hair still thick, bits of gray in the sides, not fat, skin taught on his forehead, eyes only lightly fogged, slightly pink.

I'm handsome, he mouths and wonders what picture of him they'll put in the paper. Walking from the bathroom, he notes that his throat burns when he inhales too deeply, and each breath closes with a tight small pain beneath his ribs. Crashing metal startles Ilan. His heart rate spikes. Just another truck over the steel plates at the intersection. Perspiration breaks out on his forehead despite this assurance. He spins and punches the wall hard at diaphragm height—the way you quickly neutralize someone you don't want permanently hurt. His knee involuntarily lifts with the pain in his hand. Asshole, he thinks, control your fucking fear. He shakes out his hand and inspects the small indentation his middle knuckle made in the drywall. Fucking cheap construction. Still, it bothers him to have damaged his apartment. He can spackle the wall, but he might be not have any of the tan paint.

Besides, he tells himself, you're much too lazy.

Besides, he reminds himself, what do you care?

But it bothers him.

Sometime around his fifth gin, that magic point at which Louis loses his stoic poise, he inevitably tells how the gradual corrosion of gear on Siachen—kerosene smoke coating footlockers, sleeping pads, walls, utensils, blankets in grime; snowmelt pooling on plastic floors then freezing then repooling, rusting patches on cot legs, splitting the bottoms of wood crates used as tables and stands—despite his desire to see it fall into decay, that decay would trigger an itch on his right forearm. Louis would scratch uncontrollably until he launched himself into a full-tilt panicked attempt to clean his clothes, scrub the walls, oil the footlockers and folding stools. Both responses drew his unit's ire. "It's civilization, man," Louis would say pulling up his shirtsleeve to show off the scars. "Without order, desire for order more particularly, we can't survive."

Ilan stumbles past a sewing machine triumphantly centered on a hardwood dining table, surrounded by a mélange of soiled cups and glasses, a general and his forces, a profligate and his hangers-on, a giant carp kicking up the river bottom trailed by sucker fish sifting for shit. He reaches over a granite countertop equally laden with empty take-out containers to open the cabinet in which Sonya puts the clean glasses: empty of glassware; cleanest barest spot in the house.

Ilan sighs and looks at the packet in his hand. Next to the sink, he locates the glass he believes he used to make up a batch of Morning After when he got in from Anne's place at five. At least the residue of white foam looks like it could be relatively fresh. He rinses the glass with the high-pressure Koehler sprayer, angling the glass so the exhaust spray hits the backsplash behind the sink. Held towards the light, white effluvia patterns the glass's wall like a river's delta. Ilan puts his hand on the dish-soap pump, takes it off, sets down the glass. Instead, he pulls a bowl from the cupboard and fills it with water and mixes in his Alka Seltzer.

Leaning back against the counter, legs crossed in front of him, Ilan sips from his bowl. The glazed Italian terra cotta floor tiles still shine from last week's polishing, but are littered with scraps of cloth and wire, not to mention splatters of food and drink. It doesn't matter. He can afford whatever Sonya elects to charge. He just wishes there were some way to purchase sleep. Sure, no one forced him to stay up all night drinking with Anne. No one forced him to leave her apartment immediately after they'd had sex, his ears tingling with the notion that there was something lunchmeat-like about her body. He wouldn't have slept more if he'd come home earlier; he wouldn't have slept better beside her in the bed-width alcove she screened off from her living room with bamboo-framed panels of bamboo-printed silk. A dull ache creeps from his chest into his mind-fog. It's not for Anne, he thinks. No, he hasn't lost Anne, doesn't even really want Anne. If anything, she's a response to the ache. But he can't place who he has lost. He isn't quite sure who he should call to complain about how it sucks to not be speaking. *Kvetch,* he thinks, and then: no, *kvetching* doesn't lead to reconciliation and it's a reconciliation, a homecoming, he wants.

The metal plates down in the street bang loudly and Ilan grabs hold of the counter's edge. Breathe, asshole. He inhales through his nose as slowly as possible. But the reminding of it summons the woman in Tel Aviv's face, which makes him think of the Towers—though the Towers don't really bother him per se, not in a mental hygiene kind of way. So great, he thinks, anxiety management techniques now summon anxiety. And he thinks of Louis scratching and cleaning, scratching and cleaning, scurrying between the faceless legs of men Ilan always pictures playing cards like movie-inmates in a World War Two POW camp, scratching and cleaning and waiting for the opportunity to unleash a cathartic burst of fire at movement that might be Pakistani troops on an opposite cliff face.

Of course, Ilan only learned of the cirque and the snow and the general abandonment of the area as its passes became increasingly avalanche prone later that day, after he'd finally gotten in touch with Louis, something he'd only accomplished after first booking them both tickets. But the likely tenor of their probable trip loomed with sufficient horror to make Ilan run to the men's room and kneel in a stall knowing full well the de-panted legs visible beneath the partition beside him belonged to his senior VP. As if he could have simply called Louis and said no—whether he explained the no in terms of time commitments or injury or just not wanting to didn't matter. Louis would simply remind him that Ilan had fled Israel rather than face being a hero, a hero for a deed that should be considered unquestionably heroic. Maybe he longs for the book, for

Psalms, for their abnegation. But you can't reconcile with a book. It can't hold you and love you, soothe your wounds. No, asshole, that would be your counselor's job. But Ilan doesn't have a counselor right now. And he remembers the loft bed in the loft apartment, the left support that bruised a red line at an angle between her breasts.

Ilan slurps his upended bowl of Alka Seltzer, mildly disgusted by the white sludge at its bottom. He sat at his desk, cell-phone open in his palm, as if presenting Louis' offending invitation, relayed via text messaging, to his desk for tasting. Unable to determine whether his hand trembled out of fear or general debauchery-induced debilitation, he considered fleeing to Pittsburgh or extending a leg into the Lexington Avenue traffic downstairs. He reminded himself that if he was willing to hurt himself to not go, then he might as well go and get hurt in the mountains.

Phone set down, he fondled the chunk of pink-veined granite he'd pulled out of a wall high in the Tetons on their last trip. He'd fallen forty feet clutching it before the rope caught him and brought him back in. A clean fall, it should have shown him how safe climbing was. It should have made him bolder. But when he looks closely, he can see the granite's veins throbbing. When he closes his eyes and holds it in his hands, it beats, a heart torn from the rock. It's vengeful and lovely, his tattoo's sister.

He's considered having it also tattooed on him, but it would have to be tattooed on the inside of his palm, and that's a non-starter. He can't shake new clients' hands with an angry heart stone of a palm. Sitting at his desk, he chanted objective hazards under his breath like Passover plagues: rockfall, avalanche, lighting, icefall, crevasse. Of course he wasn't brave enough to stick a leg in front of a bus either. The three and four letter symbols blinking on his monitor, Big Board and NASDAQ traded equities, eluded his focus. He picked up his desk phone to call Louis, but an image of himself listening to ring after unanswered ring froze his poised finger. Then Van Muxer's number showed on the display, and Ilan hit the button to pick up his second line. By lunch, he'd puked, bought tickets, and begun breathing normally.

Why the mountains, how not the mountains?

Waiting for Louis after work that happy-hour, Ilan slumped onto one of the Ginger Man's couches and leaned his head against the plate glass and sipped a Stella, idly imagining a car full of potash and kerosene swerving off Thirty-Fourth street and through the window. He read from a new translation of *Psalms* that his sister had sent him: *Before you bore the mountains, or you instigated for the earth and the universe; and from eternity until eternity, you: God*[14]. And after the line, Yedit Manus's interpolated musings: During the time of the void, and from one chronological infinity into the next chronological infinity, then, then which is truly a there, there, the speaker, Moses if we're to take the psalm's first line at face value, there, Moses acknowledges: You are God. And between? What about between, that vast portion of creation's topography in which time exists? Before the parting of night and day and after the return to the infinite, (before the parting of the Red Sea, and after a death in the desert), before and beyond temporal demarcation, sure, then, there, whatever: God. But between, between lies all creation bound by history, between lies us, and where in this between is God? There's an allusion to Palestine imbedded in the last word of the first half of line. The word for universe, *tevel*, can also refer to the Promised Land, and that allusion protrudes out over the precipice of the void into the space of creation, that allusion suggests God as suggested but not enacted. Let us say, then, that the suggestion of the promise of the Promised Land enacts the elision of God, His absence in the time of mountains and earth and universe and Palestine, His return only after they are turned back to dust: *tashev enosh ad-dakka.*

Ilan sets the now-drained bowl down inside of a tin-lined, copper frying pan caked with risotto residue and walks to his kitchen window. Below and between the giant oak water tanks on the roofs across First Avenue, the red and yellow crowns of Randall's Island's trees ripple beneath a perfect sky that turns the East River a false blue. Beyond, short warehouses and Astoria's uniformly six-story apartment buildings are endlessly visible, the sun already high over them. Their occupants drag themselves through showering, brushing teeth in bathrooms checked in black and yellow ceramic, thin lines of dirt fracturing hexagonal floor tiles reminiscent of Turkish baths and subway station mosaics. Ilan wishes he had toured the late nineteenth-century pneumatic-train station they'd unearthed, intact, downtown, perfectly preserved, dusty crystal chandeliers, grand piano and all. He missed the few nights it was open to the public somehow. What somehow? Surely he was out drunk looking for play. Or, having found play, was with Anne, sitting on her futon, alternately coveting the brown and red silk cover she'd sewn for it, and attempting to convince her that he couldn't live without her love in his life; then, as now.

His eyes refocus on the squat buildings far away and he imagines their exhausted tenants throwing on caste uniforms: suits and ties, bad suits and ties, hipster jeans and t-shirts beneath torn sweaters, pleated plaid skirts with high stockings and double-layered tight shirts, pointy-toed boots, comfortable shoes and polyester, elastic-waisted white pants. Ilan shivers in the small of his back, *the mountains you would bear,* what a beautiful city. Somewhere out there a black silk scarf is being knotted around two days' stubble. A low slung frontier hat. Everything is happening somewhere. Perhaps in one of the windows reflecting the morning sun's reflection off Manhattan's high-rises the Palestinian woman's brother is getting dressed.

Only inches of snow ringed the trailhead lot. Forty miles of dirt road past Boulder, Wyoming, and weather, a gray circus over the mountains, the mountains granite thrusts straight up out of the scrub dust basin, mountains that began meters east of the trailhead. A man who they'd have called a cowboy except that he rode a lama and led a train of pack-laden white goats, cleared his throat as they assembled their packs and pulled on mountaineering boots behind the rental jeep. The man brushed snow off his orange wool poncho.

"Guess I don't need to tell you there's naturals running."

"Keeps it nice and lonely," Louis answered, yanking the laces of his yellow boot propped on the jeep's bumper. "Can't turn back now, can we? We flew all the way from New York City, New York. We'll wear our beacons."

Louis switched to his other boot. Ilan's stomach rolled. Of course Louis knew about the avalanche danger before he made the plans. Their new friend began to explain that beacons didn't make avalanches safe, but Louis' look of mock wonder cut him off. Ilan wanted to take the man aside and explain...explain what? That Louis was an asshole? The guy could see that for himself. That Louis spent the better part of his twenties waiting out avalanches in a little hut at seventeen-thousand-feet on what might, or might not, end up being the Pakistani border, an extension of the red line? Instead, he finished lacing his own boots, the same Nepal Extremes as Louis.

The man whistled and his herd of mountain animals followed him off down the dirt road. Ilan noticed that the man didn't bother to wish them a safe trip. *Me'olam ad-olam, attah, El. Tashev enosh ad-dakka, va'tomer: shuvu, bnai-adam.* And Ilan regretted reading and rereading the same psalm for most of their flight, until the Hebrew had become Yedit's multiple English options, and a quiet voice repeated for Ilan alone: *From world until world, from always unto always, You, God. You retrieve man until he's crushed. You return man unto his suppression. You return man to dust. You turn man toward destruction.* To insert the mountains and their avalanches was too heavy handed for Ilan to accept, and yet, who had turned him toward the Palestinian woman that he might see in her gait, in her garb, his destruction (promised)? *You set the being towards his humiliation. You force the person's penance until he is humbled.* Crushed. Destroyed. Suppressed. Humbled. Humiliated. Crushed. *and You say: Return, b'nai-adam, the children of man, the sons of Adam.* Return where?

The veil of storm pulsed, divisive.

Louis shouldered his pack.

Ilan shouldered his pack.

Ilan will don a vest of his own regression (transgression, aggression, penance). Return to God, sure, Manus explained, or to the *adamah, to the dirt from which you were created. Ad-dakka: toward (and until) crushed.* Crushed into what? Into the earth. And a strong gust blew mountain fog around them. Then the swirling gray parted overhead. Ahead, white chutes runnelled a granite face that stretched from snow-dusted dense green to ever more clouds, *from infinity until infinity*, from avalanche starting zone to avalanche deposition zone.

Ilan whispered: Mortar and pestle. Turn me toward my crushing. You God.

"Well, Hebrew Hero, ready?"

"Why did you bother to leave Kashmir?"

"Why does that Palestinian girl's death haunt?"

"Why do I hang out with you?"

"Why does death scare you so?"

"Why do I tell you my secrets?"

"Why are you so besotted?"

"Why are you such an asshole?"

"Go fuck yourself."

"Shall we?"

And this dialogue replaced the usual: on belay? on belay; climbing? climb on. All of which is to say that of course it wasn't safe to proceed.

Even after the Alka-Seltzer, Ilan's mouth tastes vaguely of bile. His nostrils pickle as the sun reflects off the flat silver tenement roofs. His eyes well. His father is dead. Why can't Anne be enough for him? Years now, years! Years and years of convincing her to come back to him only to become quickly disgusted with her wilting, with her steady diet of vodka gimlets. She tried, for a while, early on, diligently tried, to keep up with him in his woodland pursuits. They took a trip through Harriman Park on a day like today—though earlier in the season, in October, J. Crew catalog autumn—the park wasn't large, and they chose a campsite by when she started to cry because her back hurt packing her share of an overnight's gear.

But in the morning, she loved waking to blue-sky backdropping the autumn canopy, to their spot on the hill overlooking a lake visible in stripes of light between black tree trunks. Then they hiked out—and it was only a few miles—and she began crying again.

The third time they dated, when Ilan still bothered to profess love to win her back, she tried hiking with him up Breakneck Ridge, which, for God's sakes, didn't begin to live up to its name. It had nothing in common with the K-cracks on Pingora during a snowstorm, for example. Tears. Lots of tears. Angry cursing. She punched his chest. They turned around.

Ilan pushes himself away from the window and farmer-blows through first one nostril and then the other. Fucking allergies, he thinks, staring at the snot on floor. These too can make a man wish for death. Anne has long thin fingers whose shape and translucency make him think of salamander feet. He covets their touch, has told her to treat his back as an erogenous zone. She does, sometimes, intermittently stroking and gently scratching for hours. On those nights that he falls asleep under her touch, he sleeps deeply, dreamlessly.

Yes, that's it, Ilan thinks, aimlessly opening the refrigerator while walking back to his bedroom, he's trying to gather enough new bad dreams to push the original ones out. As if the dreaming skull worked the same way as the peanut-butter grinder at the food co-op his family patronized when he was a child, and shoving extra peanuts into the hopper would force the ground dreams out. Ilan congratulates himself on his excellent psychiatric self-analysis.

He twinges for the two counselors he's seen. Well that's not really true, he corrects himself. The first woman was a nightmare. He started seeing her during his and Anne's first spell, two years after he dropped out of college and became a financial advisor—though even as recently as then, ten years ago, when he had still believed that red-carpeted floors and wood-paneled walls and framed sketches of Civil War era New York, black diagrams of fireboats and police-station maps detailing from Wall Street south inked on yellowed papers, could make him; then, when Water Street's frigid

Atlantic winter winds caught his first pair of tailored, gray Kenneth Cole suit pants below his black overcoat—the same overcoat he's been forced to wear again lately—and rippled them like a flag in a gale while he walked through 6pm-night to the after-work bars in Hanover Square, underground restaurants in which suited men paired pickled vegetables to hundred dollar wines while the narrow tall-walled streets above fell vacant; as recently as then, Ilan and his coworkers had unpretentiously called themselves stockbrokers, an accurate divide from traders, who did something else, and those who worked the floor. If they'd heard the term financial advisor back then, they would have imagined the kind of person who explained ways out of credit card debt from the far end of a toll-free help line.

Why hadn't the falafel vendor in front of New York's first police station on Water Street, who used to give free falafel-balls from his cart to whomever was waiting in line, who made falafel-conversion a religious passion, who spoke a little Hebrew from growing up in East Jerusalem and didn't mind, no, enjoyed, using it with his few Israeli customers, why hadn't he saved Ilan? Ilan thinks, why haven't I been saved? And then, but am I lost?

A truck hits the plate downstairs in the intersection, and brakes squeal loudly enough for Ilan to hear all these floors up in his hermetically sealed building, horns locked down as if heads have been affixed to steering wheels. He braces himself in his walk-in closet's doorway for the building to collapse. And how would he meet the falling ceiling? he wonders spitefully.

His first counselor was a nightmare. She worked out of her home on West End Avenue, blocks from the park and from Columbia where she'd earned (if one can call it that) her degree. During their first meetings, she nodded, taking notes, sitting in a beaten brown leather easy chair beneath an mélange of hanging plants, agreeing with Ilan that he was clearly fucked up, and for good reason, and that his behaviors were awful, but that fortunately there were ways of treating people like him. Professionals in her field had been successful with even such cases as dire as his. Then she started missing their appointments. Twice Ilan stood in her hallway, no nicer than any tenement's for all that it offered access to classic sixes: parquet floors, maids' quarters, ten-foot plastered walls ending in picture rails and crown moldings, archways and French library doors. The hallway was badly lit by small sconces, smelled stale in a way that invoked cockroaches and synagogue basement bathrooms, and was painted a dull green that blended with the brown metal doors. He knocked and knocked and no one answered. He called and got the machine. He went home. This happened for two appointments. Her assistant, who only worked rarely, claimed that she'd been sick, but why a sick person would fail to show up at home, Ilan couldn't tell.

He started seeing his second counselor after 9/11. He'd met her previously through Anne, who also saw her. They slept together twice in the woman's Chelsea apartment, and once in her midtown office. That time, in the office, she tied Ilan's arms to his chair with her pantyhose, pulled down his pants and climbed on top of him, the front of her pleated black skirt scrunched between their pelvic bones. She pushed up his shirt with the flats of her palms as she sank onto him. His tattoo, only days old, glistened beneath a Vaseline sheen and her eyes widened as she traced it with a forefinger, and then spread the gel over his body in ever widening circles while her back and breasts gradually arched away from him until she had to clamp a magazine in her teeth so as not to scream, so as not to be heard by her office mates.

Ilan walks through his closet: on one side hang suits and pants arranged black, gray, dark blue-through-light blue, seersucker, and tan; on the other side shirts range from purple to white in shades of blue. At the back, costume lighting rings a full-length mirror. His arches are fallen; a long scar crosses his left patella where he damaged his knee on a ski descent of St. Elias and then had to hike out on it anyway, eliminating any hope of orthoscopic repair. They'd had to cut him open. His thighs are strong and thick, his prick shrunken but gradually engorging as he looks at it in the mirror, his waist discolored where more than three decades of underwear elastic have rubbed on the same spot, his abdomen both hard and flabby. A consequence, he thinks, of exercise paired with drink. I'm getting stronger but looking worse, he concludes. Just left and up from his sternum the tattoo circles the spot where he shot the Palestinian woman. He traces the green ring with his left hand, holding his cock in his right hand, and the circle spreads to include his nipples, his clavicle. A tan line begins at his neck and rises to his not-yet receding hairline where skin still peels from the one day of bright sun on snow he and Louis had on the hike out from the cirque, dodging small wet slides triggered by the sudden warming, slow slush waves that pursued them at a dream-pace: slow enough to see, to contemplate, to outrun, yet sufficiently swift to catch odd ankles and draw one down to where Custer lurks beneath the quicksand.

On either side of the mirror, two drawers are built into the cabinetry. Ilan opens the left one. He picks up the closest pair of boxer briefs from the neat stacks Sonya makes each time she cleans and launders. He pulls them on and adjusts himself. He opens the top drawer on the right and takes out a pair of blue socks and puts those on as well. Sometime in his late teens or early twenties he read a novel in which a desired female proudly relates the fickle fashion in which she would discard her lovers. "Something happens, they do something, and I'm no longer attracted, I won't ever sleep with them again." One lover offended by undressing but leaving his socks on before coming to bed during an afternoon tryst. Since, which constitutes always, Ilan has made sure his socks are off his feet before naked sex. Just as surely, to refute that narrative's power over him, he puts his socks on before his clothing in the morning.

He debates wearing a t-shirt. On the one hand, he's always thought, and heard, that they ruin the lines of the dress shirt over them, especially at the waist where they impede a crisp tuck; not to mention that they often ride up over one's pants waist and poof out one's shirt. On the other hand, he reflects—using a favorite classical Greek parallel construction—there is the danger of one's nipples showing through the shirt, especially in a cold room. This debate totally ignores issues of sweat—the t-shirt both keeps one warmer, i.e. sweatier, and yet absorbs sweat, keeping the outer shirt free of pit-stains. Ilan looks in the mirror again. His nipples are hard. He's cold. He puts on an undershirt, the tattoo's green mostly visible through the stretched fabric while he pulls the waist of the shirt down; the green circle's trace disappears in wedged intervals as he buttons a magenta dress shirt over it. Ilan dons a pair of flat-fronted black slacks and a leather belt lifted from a special swinging column. From a parallel column on the shirt side of the closet he selects a gold Armani tie dotted with small purple flowers.

Ilan ties his tie with his collar turned up, looking down his nose and his chin to ensure, in the mirror, that the point of his tie covers an equilateral triangle of his belt buckle. Satisfied that it does, he pulls his collar down, enjoying the pressure of the starched, constricted cotton cutting into his neck as the crease bends in. He adjusts his knot and admires his dressed self. For a moment, the temptation to flex or adopt a fighting stance nearly overwhelms him. Instead, he smiles and smoothes the front of his shirt and pants. His hair is mussed—he hasn't showered—but short enough for him to roughly fix it with his fingers. It occurs to him that he hasn't brushed his teeth yet either. Nothing worse than leaning way out over the sink, tie over shoulder, trying not to drip toothpaste all over a shirt.

Tooth brushing is too much of an inconvenience. Ilan chews two Altoids instead, purposely rubbing the granules against his teeth with his tongue. The mint burns in what must be little cuts in his gums. Perhaps he should visit a dentist soon. Satisfied that his breath no longer stinks, Chap Stick salving his sun-cracked lips, Ilan declares himself ready. He leaves the bathroom for the bedroom. There, he opens his top bureau drawer, and takes out the drawer's only content, the vest.

A black, whitewater-kayaking lifejacket provides the vest's basic architecture. Ilan has lengthened the shoulders so that the vest's bulk hangs lower and less obtrusively. He's taken the front of a charcoal

Donna Karan vest and sewn it over the front of the life jacket. The lifejacket's buoyancy foam has been replaced with numerous short sections of PVC pipe that contain a singular mix of the crystal-precipitate of peroxide cut with acetone along with a few cartridges of butane meant for small torches, an assortment of wood screws, locking washers and wingnuts. The pipe is strung together with a magnesium-wrapped, copper wire fuse that terminates where the bulb should be in a mid-size Maglite; the Maglite, in turn, protrudes from the vest-front's watch pocket.

The vest weighs about twenty pounds.

As he has done daily these past two weeks, Ilan puts the vest on, carefully closing the underlying lifejacket's buckles before neatly buttoning the DK front. He walks heavily into the foyer under the extra weight, slips on his dress boots, and then takes the first dress overcoat he's ever bought from a stainless steel and walnut coat-rack. The coat is a size big. He's never liked it. But it fits comfortably over the vest's bulk. He's cut a slit in the left pocket that allows him to reach through to the flashlight, which he does, moving it to the coat pocket. With his right hand, he picks up the cherry-handled green leather briefcase he bought in a design store in Barcelona several years ago when he and Anne vacationed there during one of their more loving spells.

Indoors is too hot in all of his layers. Waiting for the elevator, he feels an itch climb along his underpants' bottom hem where they've crept up his thigh. Ilan inhales deeply through his nose and exhales through inflated cheeks and pursed lips, forcing pressure back into his lungs, a technique designed for exertion at altitude. The red LED display over the elevator's brushed-steel doors slowly cycles: seventeen, eighteen, nineteen—eight more floors to go. The elevator pauses at twenty-five and Ilan exclaims, sucks in his stomach, and jams a hand down his pants—not quite enough room. He undoes his belt, gets to his itch; the elevator began moving upwards. "Fuck!" He quickly pulls his hand out just in time to yank his belt tight, but not enough to buckle it, when the doors retract and unveil a woman with straight, light brown hair in a tan business suit accented with matched pearl earrings and choker.

She sighs, looks away and runs her fingers through her hair.

Ilan smiles, tight-lipped, picks up his briefcase, and steps over the threshold, careful not to look down into the space between the car and its shaft.

Women in pointy high-heeled shoes and short sharp coats hem him in as he tries to get into the Lexington and Eighty-Sixth, BMT stairwell. He grabs hold of the gloss green metal handrail, pox beneath the paint rough against his hand. He wishes for gloves. A yellow strip of grip tape running along the eroded edge of the step on which he stands doubles and then gradually becomes a single line again while Ilan stops and inhales, looking down between his dress-boots. A taller, younger, man with short, spiky, blond hair brushes past Ilan, knocking his shoulder, and disappears around the twist at the landing.

"Asshole," Ilan mutters. "I hope we end up in the same car."

But, after all, he reminds himself, the guy's just trying to get to work. He's running late; he's excited about his job, or nervous; Ilan's been there. So then, Ilan asks himself, commuters brushing against his still-stopped shoulder, constantly threatening to throw him off balance, does he want this guy on his car or not?

Why would Ilan want anyone on his car? He wishes the car empty. But then doesn't that defeat the whole purpose?

He wishes he had masturbated before leaving the house.

He hopes he doesn't blow up. Completely defeated, he trudges the rest of the way down the steps, clutching the handrail, horribly off balance.

At the top of the K cracks, the rock relaxes to forty degrees. Ordinarily, these final several hundred feet are an easy, unroped scramble. When Ilan and Louis reached them, several feet of fresh snow covered the slab, threatening to slide. Without speaking, they unroped and began kicking steps, Ilan in front. Halfway to the summit (Ilan supposed halfway, he couldn't see anything), his left foot blew out as he stepped up and right. A thick sluff entrained towards Louis. Off balance, Ilan's right foot slipped out. Amazingly, he managed to weight his axe, grab the shaft above the snow and hold on while his body punched out horizontal to the slope, emotionally vertical to the world.

His self-belay held.

His chest hit the snow, his axe held, his feet pedaled searching for purchase; and he looked over his shoulder to see Louis, hunkered down over his own axe, the snow breaking over his back and head, white against blowing gray fog deepening to purples. The sluff, several feet wide now, blew off the cliff, was caught by an up-mountain gust, and as Louis stood shaking snow off his back, the snow flew upwards as well, blew back over their heads, absorbed into the weather.

"Fucking hell!" Ilan yelled.

"We're almost there," Louis seemed to say. Ilan couldn't tell. He turned and resumed stepping upwards. He reaches the landing under the street where all the entrance staircases join, turns the corner and gets onto the main staircase to the turnstiles, limping for no reason he can discern.

Green rags in the corner speak. He tries to ignore them. The woman requests change again. Ilan has already made it down two steps of the next flight. He looks back desperately. *Turn a man*. A silver welfare cane pokes awkwardly from between and under her legs. He sighs and climbs back to the platform, reaching into his pocket. The Maglite handle rubs against his dollar-searching fingers. The pads of his fingers feel tender and swollen. Perspiration of the palms. He finds a couple of bills. The woman reaches a hand towards him. He instantly regrets coming over to her. Sprouts bloom along her skin. Psoriasis. Ilan wishes he'd worn gloves. He owns gloves: tweed-backed leather-palmed driving gloves, wool-lined Italian dress gloves in brown, burgundy and black, thick wool gloves for mucking about on low angle ice, padded knuckle, leather palmed, synthetic gloves for leading ice, bulkier yet still nimble back-country ski gloves, half-a-dozen fleece liner gloves in various weights, giant Primaloft mittens, thick rubber work gloves for dealing with chemicals and sharp wire. Crumpled in his ungloved right hand, he can't tell whether he holds a ten and a twenty or a twenty and a one. Ten is too much. Twenty is too much.

"God bless you," she says, her eyes on his hand.

She's asked that God bless him. Growing up (even after he'd grown up), whenever Ilan left his father, his father would entrust a dollar to Ilan to give to *tzedakah* at his destination. "That way, Hashem will watch over you since you're on a mission to do a *mitzvah*." He should hand her the bill; Ilan should do this *tzedakah*; he should accept this woman's blessing. The same Chasidic folklore that had his father make Ilan emissary of a *mitzvah* obsesses over the righteous disguised as the lowly. Ilan hands her the bill that might or might not have been a ten. Before he can turn away, she recognizes the denomination and grabs his hand in both of hers. He can feel the powdery dead skin, the psoriatic protrusions, dig into his own flesh. He feels her body's warmth. So warm and so stank that he thinks 'infected' and 'sewer.' Ilan wishes he hadn't thought those two words. His drawer full of gloves, neatly arranged by Sonya, calls him towards his bed.

"You're a good man," she says. "You're a good man."

Tears pool in Ilan's sinuses and he worries that he might sneeze. He pulls his hand free with a half bow, and runs down the steps. A train sits, doors open, at the platform. The pointy-toed-shoe women shove in without touching each other. Ilan's Metrocard won't read. He swipes it and swipes it again. He wonders whether he can jump the turnstile, if he can get his body to lift itself airwards or not.

A lady police officer stands next to the token booth, red hair pulled back in a ponytail under her peaked blue cap. He feels a warmth by his waist and a pull on his pants. Erection, he thinks, fucking hell. Her shirt pocket pleats bulge, rocking her nametag slightly upward. He sighs and rolls his eyes. But even so, he thinks: Those blue, blue breast pockets will pin you down. She'll feel how firm all those bulky objects are that swell your bosom.

Can she see? Can't she see? It's happening! The worst is about to happen right now! For the rest of her life she will try and remember seeing him, and think whether anything aroused her suspicions. She'll replay him over and over in her mind. She will never let it happen again. Or maybe not, perhaps his lucky streak will continue. Perhaps the bomb will not go off. Perhaps he will once again make it to work and back, gingerly managing his deadly payload.

For what though? So that he can go through this routine again tomorrow? And the next day and the next? Will she ever pin him down, her breasts crushed against his bosom's bomb?

If only he could make the leap, get over the turnstiles, turn his body on—then it would end beneath her pleats, those breasts, that nametag. Perhaps she might take him back to her apartment to interrogate him. She will strip down to her blouse, unbutton the collar down into her cleavage, her heavy-duty work bra's outline visible through both her undershirt and her light blue shirt. Or maybe she won't have on an undershirt; maybe she'll be, surprisingly, wearing a black lace bra, large enough for her breasts but cupping them so their tops rise together like an offering in the opening of her shirt.

He futilely swipes and looks back at her again; her right hand rests on her holstered billy club. Come on, Metrocard, he thinks, work. In '96 they snagged a serial rapist when he jumped a turnstile. He'd laid siege to the city's women for a week, raping a woman per borough per day it seemed. And then he hopped over a turnstile. Giuliani's quality-of-life officers arrested him, completely unaware of whom they'd caught. Down at the precinct house they ran his prints and, voila, the city's most-wanted had fallen.

The turnstile's reader chimes.

The mechanism releases audibly.

He bursts onto the platform as the train, doors shut, rocks into motion. Briefly, before its interior becomes a blur, he sees the man who pushed him on the stairway sink into a seat in front of standing coats, eye-level with women's waistlines.

The departing train leaves Ilan alone on a platform ordinarily peopled to overfilling. Behind him, the Metrocard-readers' metronomic chimes toll of an inevitable human pulse. Ilan hastens towards the platform's north end. As the spots of tar begin to form recognizable constellations between his feet, as he becomes convinced that he follows the North Star, an oblong black pox on the concrete eclipsing a ring of pink alongside the fraying yellow platform boundary that beckons towards the tunnel's strung yellow, sparkling yellow, bulbs, a north star determined, as it should be, by the handle of the little dipper, Ilan turns his eyes upwards to the walls, to the long drips of green slime sluicing down dead tile, and the pinging echo of a stalactite forming from the far corner of the platform ceiling, guarding a rotting yellow metal sheet where once there was a men's-room door. He shuffles on, lungs asthmatic, wonder-wishing whether he might not lie across the wooden bench despite its risen seat dividers. Above his forehead, the heart stone on his office desk pulses, the granite turned organ, and the thought of hands clasping his shoulders strangles him. The chimes fade as he makes distance, but he can feel the swell increase, forcing him forward, a cloud, not a cloud, a silt explosion on a clear creek bottom kicked up by a traveling foot. The Torah is water, is a stream, and if the stream is muddied...

Shema Yisraeil Adonai Eloheinu. He stops. He can't. Not out loud, not even quietly. He can't command Israel to hear; he can't declare the Lord our God is one god. The last page of Yedit's book slips into his ears: *Halleluhu bitzilteile-Shema*[15]. And her multiple translation: *Hallelujah Him with the loud symbols, Praise Him with the loud ringing sound, resoundingly praise Him with the ringing blast of the Shema; Praise him with the prayer that trumpets that He is one; Trumpet Him by trumpeting Him with a blast of the trumpet; The Lord your God is a ringing blast that the Lord your God is one.* Ilan despairs for the book in his chalice. He turns towards the tracks and tucks the case between his knees while watching a shadow become a rat become a shadow.

One night, when Louis had convinced him to come drink in

Carroll Gardens, and they were well into their sixth pint at Sparky's, Ilan discerned that the Israeli couple sitting in the booth behind them were siblings not lovers, upon which discovery, Louis asked Ilan to "come on, talk to them. Hook me up with a little Hebrew action."

"I should hook you up?"

"You're fucking a white girl. Help this American kid."

"What the fuck does Anne have to do with anything?"

"Do it."

"How are you more American than I am?"

"My father's British."

"British wouldn't make you American even if you weren't brown."

"Just speak your Hebrew."

Because they were brother and sister, not lovers, they were acceptable, because the man had suckled at the woman's mother's breast. Ilan leaned over the back of the booth's bench and found himself in a nostalgic mess of thick black curls wildly risen around his face. Maybe, he thought, (Dalia), he should start dating Jewish women again. A few words, the offer to share a pitcher of Brooklyn Pils, and the two joined them at their booth.

Almost immediately, Louis declared Ilan a hero; before Louis could explain just why that was so, Ilan offered that he'd saved Louis—for the evening at least—from the company of a climbing partner whose conversation he'd long grown sick of. Louis pinched Ilan's cheek on his way to the bar to fetch the promised pitcher. Ilan's two new friends immediately switched back to Hebrew: The girl lived in Brooklyn, her brother was traveling while he tried to figure out what to do next.

"What did you do last?" Louis asked, setting the pitcher down.

"*Medaber Ivrit?*"

"No," Louis said.

"I was the BBC's Jerusalem war correspondent."

"Seems like there's plenty of war left to cover."

"It's the same war every day. Then you find yourself sitting on your helmet eating a falafel while soldiers are shooting at the kids throwing rocks and from a building they are shooting back and then the armored bulldozer shows up and you maybe are wiping tahini from your face with a napkin but you're not actually putting the helmet back on or going behind the concrete blockage with the other reporters because yesterday and the last day you didn't do anything and you weren't killed. What there is you can do then, if not the helmet or the taking cover, is you can quit."

"We call that a negative feedback loop, and there's nothing wrong with it."

"Excuse Louis. We've been drinking."

"What's this negative feedback loop?"

"Did my blushing beauty over here tell you about the real reason the Israelites declared him a hero?"

Ilan watched a small mole above the left corner of the woman's mouth bob up and down as she alternated between smiling and frowning while Louis filled the glass she stabilized with both hands on the table in front of her. He thought about waves of young boys running up over a mound of concrete and throwing stones. He tried to visualize their individual faces; he could only summon a gray newsreel, as if he had never actually been there, as if his entire time in Israel had been spent at a table in front of one lousy café waiting for one woman in a baggy overcoat to walk down a sidewalk so that he could shoot her in the chest. (But hadn't he been waiting for Dalia? Dalia and her father? Would they ever have showed if the Palestinian woman hadn't come first? Had they stood him up? Was he there because they weren't?)

Their glasses full, Louis raised his and toasted Muslims "without whom we would have no call to armed adventure."

"Sarcastic?" the war correspondent asked Ilan.

"Once upon a time, high in the mountains, there was a glacier. On either side of that glacier, there were—"

"Never mind. I don't want to know. To Brooklyn."

Louis nodded his head, as if conceding a uniquely deft feint, and they all four raised their glasses.

"I'm not liking Brooklyn as much as I was thinking I was going to be liking it," the mole said.

Ilan nodded, agreeing that Brooklyn wasn't all that. He wondered if he could sleep with her—not so much whether she would sleep with him. That either would be or would not be something she'd do—but if it came to it, he wondered whether her particular combination of lithe and lumpy, her slightly swarthy, slightly plump, slightly barrel-chested body could turn him on. Her fingers, which initially seemed square, on closer examination, were elegantly sculpted. Of course he could get it up, he reminded himself. That wouldn't be a problem. He wondered whether completely oiling a lover's body would eradicate any sweat, or at least mask it. Louis pointed out that finding solutions to Israel's current issues must be difficult, nigh impossible. Sweat percolating through rubbing oil turned Ilan's beer sour, forcing him to concentrate on images of barley in a sunny field with powder-puff clouds and blue, blue skies to keep drinking.

"Difficult, of course difficult. But if you have ordinary people from both sides in a room, they would be finding a solution no matter how difficult. Nobody wants this. Nobody wants their children being shot by soldiers. Nobody wants bombers on buses."

"As long as you have people thinking they're going to heaven though—"

Ilan struggled to remember Brooklyn Pils' soft malty profile with crisp hops aroma but not excessive bitterness. Instead, he imagined a snow angel of body oil imprinted on his sheets, a silhouette wafting worn-polypro-funk. His fields of brown barley ears gave way to a breast sliding sideways off a torso, its aureole's nipple quivering like a soft-boiled egg's yolk. Eggs brought to mind chickens, which summoned farms, which invariably recalled his visit in fifth grade to a friend's house in the western foothills outside Jerusalem. They had lived in a beautiful Mediterranean style white house with a Spanish tile roof. While Ilan and his friend had lunched on chicken soup peppered with Osem crackers, a goat had given birth on the stone entranceway. And when they had finished eating, and stepped out to explore the local trails bisecting the farm, they had stepped around the goat, which had lain on her side and lapped casually at the placenta. Ilan's right foot cramped, seizing his bladder. He placed both hands on the table and looked to Louis in the interest of finding a break in the conversation that he might excuse himself to the restroom. Meanwhile, the reporter confessed to Louis that he did not believe in an afterlife.

"Guys," Ilan began, to no avail, while Louis' features changed and his voice dropped. "Um, guys—"

"Do you believe in God?"

"I hate to break this up but—"

"I told you I don't believe in an afterlife."

"I guess I don't either. But do you believe in God?"

"Listen, if you could just let me out—"

"Afterlife, God, heaven, deity, this is all the same thing. How are you asking about one and the other?"

Louis restated his question, ignoring Ilan. The reporter didn't seem fazed either. The mole opened her mouth and Ilan decided that if she interceded on his behalf, he would allow that she was attractive.

"Wait, now I am recognizing you."

"I'm glad you can see me now, but I have to go pee."

"Yossi, it was on *Yediot Achronot*, his face."

"I told you he was a hero."

"He is the one that's shot the bomber in front of Tam Tov."

Ilan thought he asked if he could go pee again but realized that he hadn't. His foot cramp subsided and he jiggled his leg desperately. The mole exclaimed that the shooting was a long time ago, she was just a little girl: Ilan is old. Ilan thanked her for that, and Louis finally let him out from the booth.

The lips, eyebrows, nose, chin, hair of the woman standing in front of him on the platform fail to cohere into a face so that he might attempt to discern whether he in fact does know her as she claims, or whether her claim is a spurious as it seems. Having, at least temporarily, arranged her features, *tashev enosh,* Ilan searches them for landmarks, *harim yuladu,*[16] that might jog his memory. Instead, he remembers the white cat, who, on account of her ears, his parents use to joke was a Russian robot spy. He loved the cat, a stray, fed it on a paper plate in their small Pittsburgh backyard until winter and his parents' refusal to let him bring it inside, but that doesn't help Ilan place the fading features facing him.

"McCools, last Thursday. I got my hair cut?"

"No. Of course, of course. You live in the building next door."

"Around the corner."

Ilan tries to undo what he supposes must be a leer, but his new assortment of facial expressions feels too much like a scowl. Maybe leering isn't so bad. She doesn't seem to mind. He thinks they made out in the back corner booth. In fact he's completely certain of it. For that reason, he hasn't taken Anne to McCools for the past several days, scared that some drunk regular—the sanitation workers who drink from midnight till their shifts start at 4am, a perfect overlap with bar closing time—will either rat him out or blackmail him. He remembers the texture of this woman's breast against his fingertip calluses, the underwire of her bra pressing against the back of his wrist, while they stood, her mouth in his, in front of her building, where she did not invite him up, but insisted on him entering her number into his cell phone, from which he could theoretically call her, were there any chance of his remembering her name.

An itch forms along the surface of his upper body, a tingling along all of his skin, the leading indicator of perspiration's opening salvo. Ilan regrets wearing a t-shirt after all. He wishes the avalanche that knocked Louis seventy meters down a slope towards the beckoning Siachen below, forcing him to ice climb back to his small base—to the single metal and plastic hut, with its few machine guns and mortar, its fourteen men—forcing Louis to ice climb, barehanded, permanently damaging the circulation in his hands, Ilan wishes the avalanche had simply knocked Louis over the cliff band that began mere meters below the moment of Louis' self-arrest. Ilan can't quit tell whether the heat is affecting his digestive and nervous systems, or whether his presumption that the heat will is affecting them. Or, perhaps, his digestive system and nervous system are generating the heat causing him to perspire. He feebly asks the McCool's woman whether she's headed to work, only to cut himself off and comment on what a stupid question that was, obviously she is.

"Actually to Penn Plaza to take my Series Seven."

Tensed pulses develop into direct communications between the muscles over Ilan's eyebrows and those within his abdomen. *Baruch sheim kavod malkhuto l'olam va'ed*, the second line of the *Shema*, whispers across his lips, and it is meant to be recited in an undertone, and he hopes his whisper was not aloud. He hopes that he might have accidentally said something about the Series Seven exam instead, something friendly, something that implied commiseration.

She lightly punches him in the shoulder, but from a full boxer's stance, chides him for not calling.

Ilan supposes one could find her relatively cute in a short feisty generic kind of way. Why the hell would anyone want him to call? He wouldn't mind seeing her body naked (to imagine it clad in the blue pleats of the policewoman, the baggy black of the Palestinian woman). He doubts if he would remember her nude form any better than he remembers her name. That doesn't matter. The hot flashes running up and down his spine matter. A building rush of warm wind anticipates the rough metal gushing of an approaching train and the woman asks whether he'd had a hard night: he seems distracted.

"No, sorry. I'm just remembering that I forgot my laptop. Trying to decide whether I really need it or not."

"Come on, you don't need it."

"Well I'm giving a presentation to a client later."

"Like you haven't done a million of those."

He looks at her again. She's young is what she is. Young and Jewish and eager. She'll fuck him if he buys her a bottle of wine in the tiled antechamber of an underground restaurant she didn't know existed, takes her for a walk in the lilac-ed dusk of the

Botanical Gardens, lets her imagine herself spying on him and their baby playing crash with desk ornaments on the floor of his study in a big old farmhouse somewhere up the Hudson.

And she'll sit next to him on the train and talk for the fifteen minutes down to Thirty-Fourth Street.

She'll make him want to explode and he'll feel nostalgia for his own people and he'll feel anxious and become disgusted at how generic she is and he'll feel the desire to marry her and buy a house in Bethpage and raise a family and grow a short beard and start selling 403(b)(7) accounts to school teachers. He'll yearn to grow a short beard and wear frumpy sweaters beneath faded blazers and raise a family in Bethpage or Garden City or Teaneck and bring boxes of donuts and cartons of coffee to public school break rooms and after school chase hesitant teachers potential clients to their cars in the teachers' lot weighted with plastic grocery bags full of marketing materials four-color brochures trifolds CD-ROMs swinging from his hands. The subway's headlights gleam along molten rails, moments from the platform.

"No, I do need it. Very big."

Ilan runs back towards the turnstile, shoving his way through firm wool, battling through the overstuffed compression of commuters. Behind him, barely audible over the train, the woman yells to call her.

To call her! He shudders, knees shaking beneath the weight of his thighs; he wants to call her, and he shudders again and bursts through the turnstiles. Back to square one! Off the platform, a second train missed.

No way he'll be on time to work. So much for talking to Jerry Thomson about Pfizer options before opening bell.

Gas presses against his bowels and he stops before the handrails, back arched, to let his sphincter relax. The lady cop reclines against the token booth's bulletproof glass—no hoodlums would get a chance to set that one alight—glances at him offhandedly. No doubt she thinks he's an idiot. No way he can fart here. He scurries back up the stairs, his limp magically gone, the aboveground air crisp and cool; he inhales and his lungs feel functional. For Christ's fucking sake, he was reciting the goddamn *Shema* down there. Is he so close to it, to declaring God?

Sure, he doesn't have to fart now, now that he's above ground, but he knows that the gas is in his system, hiding out somewhere. As soon as he descends, it'll come back. Better to try and force it out. He hiccups lightly out of fear that the forcing might lead him to shit his pants.

Ilan passes a take-out sushi shop and a designer tie boutique and a wine store full of backlit ovals that specializes in bottles less than twenty dollars, all the while contracting his lower abdomen. Nothing doing. He sighs and turns back towards the train entrance. With any luck his body will cooperate for the next twenty minutes. If he'd simply put up with the woman, gotten on the train, assumed that the wave of body angst was just that, a wave, a flash, a fading temporary, then he would be practically to work by now, five minutes from the full safety of his restroom-equipped office. If he'd just asked the Palestinian woman to sit for a coffee. If Dalia: her black ringlets and her bent-neck laugh and her parents' clean house full of thick white carpet. If. Instead, the whole ride, the entirety of underground time still lies ahead of him. He fondles the flashlight's pebbled handle. His life lies in front of him, what's in front of it, never knowing. Or he could just blow himself up as soon as he gets on the train. Maybe that's the time to do it, when the gas pains become overwhelming, he'll detonate. Or the undoubtedly unstable mixture sloshing around the PVC piping in his vest may elect to blow him up when he least expects it. As long as any accidental detonation doesn't happen at work: he knows those people; those people deserve better. (Doesn't everyone? God wants what he wants Ilan doesn't want a bomb.) Two steps down towards the platform he pauses, and finally passes gas, loudly.

The couple below him in the stairwell snickers, snickers and then laughs, their heads close together, their legs tripling speed.

A flush rushes up from his neck and Ilan mumbles an apology he doubts anyone can hear. He gives the couple a few seconds to get sufficiently ahead of him. They probably don't know who they heard anyway. It isn't like they'd looked back and up.

He feels better.

The homeless lady blesses him again and he thanks her, his pleasure at his ability to respond naturally and confidently measured in the width of the berth he gives her hands.

He continues on to the turnstile and tries to swipe his card. Nothing doing. He once again considers jumping it, and though the day seems brighter, if only twenty minutes later, and lighter, if only due to shedding weightless gas, he refuses to believe he can muster the necessary vertical. The green led reader displays, denied, which makes no sense given his monthly-unlimited pass. He tries a fourth time, same thing, and wonders what to do. A loud "Sir" comes from behind him. This is it. The hand will clasp his shoulder. "Sir," again, and again, "excuse me, sir."

Reluctantly he turns around to face the lady cop.

"Sir, it won't work if you've used it less than twenty minutes ago."

She had noticed him and recognized him. *Me'olam ad-olam, attah El.* He wonders if she heard him fart, if she knows it was him that farted.

"I thought I forgot some papers and I had to run out."

"Ok, sir, but it won't work twice in twenty minutes."

"I have a monthly unlimited."

"You're not listening to me, sir. I'm saying that the reader doesn't let you use the pass twice in twenty."

"I paid. Seventy-three dollars I paid. I should be able to ride the subway to work."

"I'm not trying to argue with you."

"What am I supposed to do?"

"You can talk to the station attendant."

"The station attendant?"

A train pulling in drowns out the lady cop's words, but nothing in the *tevel* could disguise her look. He cups one ear with a hand and points back with his thumb. He considers turning the Maglite on, but quickly rejects that idea. The lady cop taps the token booth glass over her shoulder with her billy club. So the station attendant is the token booth clerk. Well how was he supposed to know that? Why the hell couldn't she have just said 'token booth clerk' anyway? He lifts his hands to mock his own stupidity, and gets in line behind the couple who laughed at him. In front of them, a flower-patterned plastic rain bonnet bobs to the clerk lecturing her on the central Metrocard office's provision of senior citizen passes so that seniors don't have to come to the booth each time and pay cash. The train doors chime. Three trains he's missed. What a morning. He'll never make it to work.

The old lady walks away, head still bobbing like one of those dancing Coke cans, and the couple advances. Why couldn't they use the automatic machines? Why did they have to delay his ride? He has a monthly-unlimited. Asshole, he chastises himself, you've got time till the next train arrives. You'll make it fine. He wonders at how the volume thins past nine-fifteen. So much for trading at the opening bell. So much for those Pfizer options and Jerry and everything. Pharmaceuticals, investment; investment in the right to invest, that's what options are. Talk about outside of the creation, of things. Whatever. He's told his clients before that they aren't in the day-trading business; a security's movement over years, not minutes, should excite them. Options purchases ought to be to hedge risky and short-term holdings against any sudden movements he might miss because he can be out to lunch as easily as late to work, because of situations like this, (situations in which he's hung over and wearing a vest that's a bomb; the options will hedge against whatever volatility in his absence, including that volatility caused by his volatile vest; how wise of Ilan, how considerate he is of his clients, to ensure that their finances don't suffer the suffering of others). Still it's a matter of perception, being punctual or tardy—he could always fake a breakfast meeting with a prospect.

He is so close to the lady cop. Saliva glistens along the ridges of her parted lips and he can see the slight gap between her two front teeth behind them. Her chest rises fast and shallow; this must be a response to his scrutiny, as is her forward stare, not acknowledging him. He wonders what would happen if he pulled her in by her waist and kissed her. He wonders what would happen if he pulled the Berretta out of her hip holster and began shooting.

A Berretta! He has a bomb!

The clerk asks Ilan how he can help him. Ilan explains his situation. The clerk swipes his card in his reader and sees that it's valid. Ilan complains that he really doesn't think that he should have to buy a second fare when he already has a monthly pass and simply forgot something and wasn't trying to do anything he wasn't supposed to or get anything he wasn't entitled to.

"Relax yourself, sir. I'll buzz you in."

"Buzz me in?"

"Go to the door, sir, and I will buzz you in."

"The door?"

"Yes, sir. The door."

Ilan thinks to walk around to the token-booth door and then realizes that has to be wrong. "Excuse me for being an idiot, but which door do you mean?"

"The one that the strollers go though, sir. You all right?"

"Of course, where the strollers go though. Silly me."

Ilan pushes open the grated metal door next to the turnstiles. Idiot, asshole, he thinks, do you want to draw attention to yourself? Think! For the second time this morning, Ilan wishes that Louis had met his end in the shrapnel geyser of an errant Pakistani mortar. Of course, wishing doesn't make it so. Of course, Ilan could simply leave the station again, take off the vest, refuse to go on any more climbing trips, break up with Anne, stop drinking, move cities, start golfing—and what? Would the erasure of the tattoo on his chest somehow erase with it the gun and the lilt in her left eye and the way the advertisement for Time cigarettes on the bus behind her went out of focus as he sighted on her chest?

Where is the spot where he was standing on the platform? Ilan probes his lower chest for the tattoo. The green ink pulses through the vest, through his shirt, his vest, his coat. And why does he need to be in the exact same spot anyway? Ilan measures distance from the burgeoning stalactite before assuming a stance exactly half a meter back from the yellow boundary tape, idly caressing the tattoo's ridges. This'll do, he decides, half expecting the woman to reappear.

He looks down at the left hand that touched her breast. Sure enough, calluses give a plastic hardness to the tips of each finger. He should be able to climb just fine with these hands. Fucking Louis. Perhaps, Ilan thinks, there is God without heaven. Perhaps Louis is right. Can he read Manus' psalms that way? Perhaps. Perhaps, perhaps, perhaps: everything is perhaps; anything is possible. Or if, always if: anything was possible. Perhaps and If, two friends. Fuck it. It's possible the moshiach himself, the goddamn messiah, in the flesh, will show up later this morning on a white donkey, in midtown Manhattan, blowing the other horn from the goat slaughtered in Isaac's stead on Mount Moriah and that all the dead will then roll through underground tunnels back to Israel. Perhaps. *Praise Him with the blast of the shofar*[17]. Her translations lack comfort, continuously force him back out of divine recourse and into the world in which he needs recourse to the divine. They are the opposite of climbing, which, once he actually begins the movement of, leaves partner and ground below, erases the world and transports him to a calm afterlife.

He climbs towards heaven! And the sarcasm in her translations is so pronounced that all she has to write is 'Praise Him' to point out the problem of God. Her translations draw him towards them, make him long for them, for their comfort, but as soon as he begins reading them the comfort summoned disappears, the world comes into sharp, harsh focus. That's it, Ilan decides. He'll throw the book in the tracks.

He turns towards the tracks, lining both toes up on the yellow line. What, is he at the starting line of a race? Ilan asks himself, and answers, perhaps. Again with the perhaps? Perhaps everything! Nothing changes. That's the whole point. *Halleluhu bitziltzele teruah. Kol haneshamah tehallel Jah, hallelujah*[18]. In the last lines, they praise God with *teruah* on the shofar. Then, after that, it's the future tense, *every being will praise Jah*. The moshiach comes in the present tense, but it's only in the future that everyone praises him, which is to say, that only in the future does the Moshiah's promise lead to anything: the Rabbi Schneerson probably was the moshiach after all, and the Lubavatchers are right to stand around his grave drinking tea and praising *his* name; and that future, in which all beings praise God, is *Hallelujah*, which is to say: *Baruch Hashem*, which is to say: with God's blessing, which is to say: per-fucking-haps, which is one goddamn perhaps that's guaranteed to mean definitely not at all. Or, in other words, he's going to get on the fucking subway train with his homemade, unstable, mother-of-fucking-Satan-fueled bomber vest.

Ilan realizes he can see his hands in front of him because they have been gesturing wildly.

He puts them down and rubs his palms along the sides of his overcoat. In the process, his case slips down from between his knees onto the platform, falling perilously close to the edge. He leans over to pick it up, and a train rushes into the station, the flashing metal sides inches from his hair. He considers leaning forward, a technique even more effective than committing the book to its destruction on the tracks (*tashev sefer ad-dakka*), he's already largely memorized; better to commit the head that contains *Psalms* to the tracks (*tashev enosh ad-dakka*). He immediately thinks better of killing himself, and instead stands up, the swimming black spots obliterating images of rescue by beautiful station personnel, the lady cop stripped down to lace panties and bra, her abdomen taut even when she leans over him, compressing his chest, her peaked cap askew.

Gradually the face-flashing windows slow sufficiently that Ilan can make out the individual passengers. The train is less crowded than the one he usually rides. Peopled mostly, no doubt, by those who commute late to avoid prime target hour. In fact, there's a reasonable chance that he can score a seat, though he rejects that idea as too awkward; he's a bomber after all, however unlikely; he should stand, it's the least he can do. He reaches into the inside pocket of his overcoat and pulls out his Blackberry. Ilan hits send to call Louis before remembering that the phone won't work in the subway. If he wants Louis to explain the very small dimension in which the constants defining life's most perplexing questions—the exact location *and* speed of an electron—he'll have to wait until he gets off the train. Or he could go back up the stairs again and make a call before going to work. The thought of yet another cycle with the turnstiles turns his stomach, which turns him towards the exit.

The train doors open and a flush of commuters press around Ilan driving him forwards into the nearest car. Stop! he suddenly, desperately, doesn't shout: Don't get on! This train goes to the camps!

And the very fact of the thinking threatens to mean that today he will scatter himself on his wingnuts and old bolts and strips of plastic. Or, and he searches the passengers to see this, perhaps a terrorist is on the train—it makes sense that there would be, should be, come on already, how could a terrorist not have attacked the trains yet? A dark skinned man in a baggy down jacket catches Ilan's focus until he greets a woman in Spanish inside the car. Ilan laughs at himself: how many bombs do you think there could be on one train anyway, asshole? He can't deny it, there's a real relief in being the guy with the Maglite actuator in his pocket.

The doors shut behind Ilan and he grabs on to the center-post. He begins calculating dispersion angles by estimating his distance from the doors. This car being at least two generations old, refurbished most recently to install modern air-conditioning—which is not turned on today, he notes—and once earlier to make the interior graffiti-proof—despite which, various tags are etched into the plastic windows and scrawled on the advertisements over the handrail—means that he's about four feet from the door. If he walks to the next pole down, he'll be nine feet from the door he entered through and about twelve feet from the door at the end of the car. Move your feet, asshole, he tells himself. And why take these additional steps?

Overhead, Dr. Zizmor, gray-skinned and white frocked, smiles down at him, a rainbow arching from behind his head encircles bulleted services: acid peels, acne-treatment, laser-birthmark-removal.

Leave me alone, Dr. Z, Ilan thinks, hopefully not aloud, and begins shuffling sideways down the car to the next pole. He grabs for the pole but a brown glove is already there, he reaches lower, which feels awkward for his arm. He wants to wrap the crook of his elbow around the metal, but then he'd be leaning against other people's hands. Don't do that.

He reaches higher, but the brown glove slides up the pole as well.

He quickly darts below the glove. Yes, perfect hand height!

The brown glove slides down to rest on his hand. At the top of Pingora, Ilan found himself saying the *Shema* as he imagined the double rope ends blowing back up the mountain when they cast them down to rappel. The rope ends blown above them and tangled on rocks and no way to get down through the teal and purple wind, through the incumbent lightening. Hashem, Ilan promised, Hashem, to whom Ilan had not made promises since his night with the orange-haired colonel. Hashem, if you just let me get down from here, I'll never read Manus's book again. Louis turned back to him, his cheeks rippling in the wind as he tried to speak the way a young Ilan's suit pants had in lower Manhattan.

Louis laughed and walked next to Ilan, cupped his hands around his mouth and yelled into Ilan's ear, his voice chopped by the wind, "God is an algorithm for wind, for snow, for coefficients of friction and probabilities of avalanches. You can't beseech him. He's a constant."

Then a rainbow spanned a crack in the cumulus and Ilan remembered God's covenant with Noah, that He would not destroy man ever again. *Because a thousand years in your eyes, like a day yesterday that's already passed, v'ashmurah balayelah*[19]. Does God's sense of time make memory or defeat it?

The clouds beneath Pingora's summit seemed so thick that Ilan imagined he could jump and be carried off. If Hashem isn't bound by time, then didn't His agreement with Noah, sealed by that man's traversing the chopped carcasses of the additional kosher animals—goats and cows, of which he brought eight each onto his ark for this explicit purpose: to sacrifice six—didn't that agreement apply retroactively, to all time if any time, as time is a place for Hashem, not a progression. Stop the climb, he thought. *balayelah: in the night*. But Ilan was already at the top of the climb; stopping the climb could only be effected by descending. And in the night, man might be pounded into the ground from which God bore him.

Why was it that Louis could stand upright, tie the ropes together, approach the edge, over which they must rappel, with confidence?

Ba-lay-ye-lah, balayelah.

He spoke the word aloud.

Take me, Yedit, take me, Ilan shouted to the contracting rainbow. He imagined her as the disembodied head of Charlton Heston's Moses, long white beard flowing down from heaven. He tried to force himself to see her as a woman, if for no other reason than to distract himself from the cold, from the fact that Louis clearly relied on the air's force to hold him upright as he leaned over their rappel path. At best, he could summon an El Al flight-attendant: he tried to latch onto her image, but doing so painted deep purple mascara cuts beneath her eyes, bleached hair frizzing from beneath her peaked cap, thighs genetically designed to push wooden carts laden with horseradishes down a cobble Warsaw street, or bear (*yuladu*), in a deadlift, the combined sorrows of the defeated generations likely to spring (*teholel*) from her loins.

Fall! he commanded Louis.

Don't fall! he commanded Louis.

Would that it were the thick-thighed woman in a black sack pushing a wooden-wheeled cart that finally said: Enough! Would that it were her that psalmed an answer to Dovid HaMelech that freed her offspring from the shackling faith that kept them bent over archaic Aramaic texts while their assassins approached with boots and guns and gas chambers.

Enough!

No more fighting guns with prayers and Halakha and Talmudic understanding: God is a shout that He is God!

(Would that when Ilan shot with a gun his would-be assassin that act had unshackled him.)

Without a stone and a sling, Dovid could not have slain Goliath. Did Louis' infinitesimally small dimension full of constants, just big enough for numbers, house God or constitute God? Ilan clipped his Reverso to the rappel loop on his harness and held it out in front of him, which pulled his hips forward. He swayed in the wind. The Reverso's two metal boxes came out of alignment and then slid back into it. They couldn't possibly hold his rope and if they didn't—*v'ashmurah balayelah: and a night-watch in the night.* Three to four hours in the night are a watch in the night are a night-watch, *ashumurah;* from *shomer*: to guard, to defend, to uphold, to wait, God before the mountains, and a day, yesterday, was like a thousand years. A thousand years: like hours in the night. A thousand years: more than the years between Noah's flood and Moses' birth, almost exactly the time between the first day and Noah's birth. From creation to destruction is only a thousand-year-cycle for the speaker of the psalm, Moses if the first line is to be believed, and that is but three hours in the night in God's eyes (closed for the night), maybe four hours.

Before the universe and after eternity, You, God, and between them an *ashmurah*, the hope of creation, Ilan, like three hours in the night; God a suggestion of a pun on *universe*, a *tevel's* allusion to Palestine .

The entire Zizmor family captures Ilan's gaze, the entire Zizmor family who applaud New Yorkers on their heroism after September Eleventh, behind them a range of purple mountains. Survival isn't heroism! he wants to shout. We were dumb cows walking down a staircase. Getting worked up about 9/11 annoys him. Sure him too, but his is different. His is being interviewed on Army Radio and mumbling about the hiccup the woman made when he shot her and the interviewer taking his eye out from behind the camera to look at Ilan. A red ring ran through the interviewer's eyebrow and across his cheekbone where the eyecup had pressed. The man blinked and for a moment he wasn't an interviewer, but one of the young boys Ilan had known in *kitah daled*, fourth grade, when his parents took him to Jerusalem for a year, boys who watched Ilan secretively throw away the hard-boiled egg from his lunch each afternoon because he didn't want it, yet was the only boy in school wealthy enough to waste food, watched him like they would watch the decay of an empire of which they wanted no part, like one would watch a suspected avalanche path from a safe vantage in anticipation of its slide.

The flashlight handle sticks to Ilan's hand. He realizes that he's sweating, wishes, once again, he'd worn gloves. Why do you wear this vest every day? Ilan asks himself. When once, early in the planning stages, he mentioned the possibility of blowing up a train to Louis, Louis had suggested that this was typical survivor's guilt, or victim's guilt, depending upon how you wanted to cut it—and, three gins into another fine evening down at the Divine Bar, Louis wanted to cut it both ways. Of course Ilan wanted to become his victimizer, and therefore, he'd come to agree with the rightness of his vicitimizers, the terrorists in Israel, the terrorists who flew planes into the Trade Towers. Likewise, Ilan believed his survival made him an adversary of those who had not: most who sat at a metal table at a sidewalk café were not turned towards the Palestinian woman who approached them, did not fire at her, did not live past her last act. That Ilan had made him not like them, and if was not like them, then he must be of those who killed them. Three thousand of the people who worked in Ilan's office building died. "It's natural, buddy, that you'd contemplate these things," Louis concluded. "Easily explained."

Asshole, Ilan had wanted to reply, you don't fucking know me.

"What's more," Louis resumed. "The brain is bound by physics. Your responses are neurologically predetermined. If one could devise the appropriate algorithm, and insert the appropriate constants, one could show exactly how expected your responses are."

"Don't tell me that my psychology can be explained by your weensy freaking dimension with its seventeen numbers or whatever."

"That dimension is God. Of course it can explain you."

"God exists to provide an afterlife. Plus, if your God is just these numbers, then he can't have spoken to Moses or to Abraham or to any other man. Therefore, there is no God in the world in which your little freaking dimension is God."

"I concede that my God's dimension is too small to contain an afterlife."

"Then it's not God."

"The constants determine the encounter with wonder which leads to the conclusion that there is God. From them inexorably extends the evolution of the human need for deity, including the need for an afterlife and the need to reject that afterlife as necessary, or as moral imperative."

"Might as well not exist at all."

"Yes God; heaven no."

"It's depressing."

"Hey," Louis said, "I'm not accountable for that."

Ilan strokes his left side with his left hand feeling for the tattoo. His right shoulder aches from holding onto the railing too low down. Still, he looks at Zizmor's family. Straight out of Queens, he thinks, straight out of Long Island. And where is he from? Pittsburgh? Israel? Brooklyn? The Upper East Side? Does that make him such a big *macher* that he's got something over these people? No, but he hates the Zizmors, who smile at him when he least wants to see smiles. He forcefully breaks his eye contact with the elder Z. He feels the train's sway as it sways towards walls covered in swathes of colored text, serpent-tailed metallic lettering briefly lit by the car's window, as if the train was a scanner of lost text painted by primitive peoples, as if the train, like the Beis HaMikdosh, had windows designed to shine light out rather than let it in.

Could all this writing date back to the Eighties? How brilliant the colors remain.

He imagines leaving the smoking husk of a train and wandering back up the tunnels to the nearest emergency exit, light filtered through street level grates illuminating lost treasures painted on the concrete blocks between steel ceiling beams. (This would only happen if some other bomb-bearer's bomb exploded; Ilan will not survive his own detonation.) Young men must jump off the edge of the platform and wander here and between passing trains spray these elaborate glyphs. Work gangs swinging plastic lanterns and four-foot long wrenches for the track-tie bolts must pursue them. Always the worker chases the witch (the serf: the Jew).

But the swaying of the metal tube in which he rides makes Ilan dizzy. He defines subway car as a place one cannot leave until it reaches a station, or as a device for traveling through a kind of no-man's-land inhabited by rats and mole-people. Mole people, please, he chides himself. If you're not strong enough to look out the window, asshole, then don't look out the window.

Ilan reaches down to his briefcase to take out Manus' book, in the process lowering his gaze to rest on the woman seated beneath the window. The psalms' beauty stems from the agonizing pace of their translation, the weight on every line. Of course the words become only words. The Doctor Zizmor ad: clear, and face, and acid, and peel and skin and treatment and heroism and heroism and applaud and skin and applaud and applaud and New Yorker, skin applaud New Yorker. Clear can mean the sky or glass or transparency or obviousness. Ilan could drag his teeth along the raised arch of the woman's right cheekbone. Yes, any words read slowly enough, transposed sufficiently laterally carried past the tunnel and the graffiti and the metal poles and the fluorescent bars of light behind the advertisements and the stacked concentric circles of the overhead air vents, yo-yoing down, ever down, every word read, every word written, denied, proved, makes irrevocable the impossibility of, *He will kiss me with his mouth's kisses*[20].

Ilan's lungs fill with more air than they can hold; breath breaks tingling channels between his ribs, bursts through to his skin. And he inhales again. He inhales again. *Ki tovim dodeyikh mi'yayin. Because your loving is better than wine.* Ilan can't help thinking that *daled*, with that *daled* it could be mistaken for breasts; he can't help wondering where those kisses were meant to land.

The top lid of her left eye extends slightly past the lower, black lashes extend the line further so that her eye tapers endlessly towards her neck.

Mashcheni: seize me; inhabit me; Ilan wants to inhabit the enunciation: *ma-se-ke-ni! Draw me; possess me; prolong me. Mashcheni achareyakh.*

A flush creeping up Ilan's chest assures him that she would let him bring his tongue from the dip of her nose across her eye, that she would arch her back as he tasted the gold-flecked curvature between her lids.

Achareyakh: behind you.

Mashcheni achareyakh: seize me into your wake, inhabit me, prolong me along behind you. Bring me along after you. Possess me. Mashcheni. (Your loving better than wine; better than wine, those kisses from the kisses of your mouth.)

Ilan brings his briefcase in front of his coat and clutches it to his chest with both hands to prevent himself from brushing a thumb across the invisible hairs corner-sprung of the lips of her mouth. *Narutzah: We'll run.* The words are so small. They are so individual. If only these words, *Shir haShirim,* were in Yedit's book. If only he could open it now and find:

We will remember your loving more than wine.

Solomon!

Solomon, whose loving do you long after that it would draw you behind? (This woman's breasts, Ilan wants to say, transfixed, as unable to define her as the bible is unable to describe Sarah or Bat Sheva or Esther. If this woman before him is not altogether a phenomenon beyond words, then she is at least Ilan's ineffable encounter.) And the words are so small, so small that they seem to exclude God and when she inhales her nostrils flare and her eyes half shut, her chest rises slightly in its buttoned-up, wide-collared jacket. And there was Esther as well as the thick-thighed woman pushing horseradish. But somehow Esther always ends up with Nebuchadnezzar and the peasant in the babushka selling roots to support her husband swaying over illicit transcriptions of God's unspoken word documented in Babylon—yes, the peasant woman is the one who bears the race, who brings baby after baby into the world, who works to let her anemic *chazan* sport a streimel and rejoice in the love of the Lord. And it is her that must shave her head and hide it beneath a wig, as if the Cossacks ready to rape wouldn't already be disgusted by the stout swaddled ridges of her varicose calves!

And the Esthers give themselves to Persian kings!

I am but a lily shoot yet of the Sharon; am a lily, full on, in bloom, of the valleys. Like a lily between thorns is my delight between the daughters.[21] Inhale and exhale: coarse bits of subway soot threaten his throat's integrity.

When he translates 'valleys' from Hebrew, from *amakim,* the space between the languages summons the word's imagery: expanses of evergreens hiding small blue pools hemmed in by sunned-sage-scent, concavities of gray scree stretched up to bands of snow binding the bases of granite cliffs thousands of meters high. And after he translates *rayati: delight, beloved companion,* he loses *amakim's* echo of shepherds and the pastures in which sacrifices-to-be are set to graze.

I could have lived in Prague! Ilan marvels. I could have worn button-on collars and black suits. I could have married this woman with her round-toed brown Mary-Jane shoes and we would have had a flat and drank espresso and Tokai wine, shaded from the sun by striped yellow awnings hung from winter-stone buildings.

He inhales and when he's taken in so much air that the blood bursts out of his lungs into his flesh, into his crotch, he tastes a tincture of African hyena musk and wilting crocus and the barest hint of something like dusk observed from a tiled terrace, lilaced over the summer Nile. He knows this is her: Nile mank beneath the perfume and Italian green leather gloves and lavender shampoo.

She is Bat Sheva's son's delight amongst the daughters.

Ilan thinks about his cock because he sees this woman and remembers Anne's mouth around his penis last night coaxing it almost hard enough to force into her body when she climbed on top of him, tried to contain him, draw him in. *Inhabit me. Your loving more than wine.* There is a line in the skin around Anne's neck that mostly disappears when she tilts her chin upward.

He shakes his head and takes one hand off the briefcase to feel the flashlight.

At any moment the sliding door between cars could rip open, the lady cop could come running through, having searched car after car looking for him, something about his dazed reentry triggering a suspicion she couldn't leave rest long enough to call for back-up. Once again he imagines her pinning him. Once again he tries to imagine her naked. But she is sanitized now, her flesh rendered clean. On top of him, her breasts recede into flexed pectorals, her abdomen hardens, the tattoo appears over her sternum. Ilan shivers and fondles the flashlight's button, shuddering along his neck. He can't quite summon the lady cop's face. Nor can he dispel her chest. Instead, he sees a dusk image beneath her cap with his nose protruding from it. He can picture the red bra, but can't exactly get it to stick onto the body. He can make female breasts appear, but musked with rancid powder. Roller-ball deodorant. Sweat-grimed city soot. The black buttons on the woman's jacket undulate with her breathing. She becomes fragments of moving fabric; Ilan flinches backwards, worries that he's jumped backwards, realizes he's only moved millimeters, realizes she's only reaching down into a thick-stitched purple saddlebag tucked between her knees. The car's wheels roll across the rails like the sound of crushing slate as the train rounds a curve coming into the fifty-ninth street station. Four more stops to go.

The doors open. A woman pushes a stroller on. A man leaves his Financial Times next to a patch of white where the gray laminate has peeled from the bench. Ilan prays that the woman in front of him will not get up. The man sitting behind Ilan stands up and walks to the door but doesn't get off the train. The woman remains seated as the doors close, her book clamped between the flats of her forearms and her pressed-together legs. Ilan exhales and the muscles in his lower back relax. His eyes tear, refracting orange bands around the station lights. He wishes he hadn't wished the woman on the train. He wishes he'd wished her safe and off. Asshole, do you think your prayer kept her on the train? Either she was going to get off anyway or not. It's not as if, even if there were a god, that god made her change her mind so that she would ride the train for while. When the Palestinian woman walked towards the café, Ilan knew that it was her, the one he must shoot; he had crossed his legs to give his left elbow a higher resting point—that of his right knee—before sighting and firing. Well sure, Ilan acknowledges, Hashem, may he exist, would not likely have changed the mind of this woman reading before him in answer to the prayer. But, since Hashem had already experienced Ilan's prayer—all man's prayers and deeds existing outside of time and therefore simultaneously already before God—then he might have answered the prayer before the woman ever got on the train. God could have created the woman such that one sunny November day she would ride this particular car of the nine-fifteen train to work and that work would be sufficiently far away to necessitate her overlapping with his ride. Does that then mean that Hashem wants Ilan to blow up this woman? Well, asshole, Ilan thinks, you've been riding this train wearing this vest for what, two weeks now? Maybe this Hashem of yours simply wants her to be in proximity of a bomb. Maybe you won't have to detonate today.

Ilan's tear ducts tingle but do not well over.

Sure, in a world in which Hashems plan all these things out, that's also a world in which the unacknowledged presence of a bomb touches the fucking soul, and somehow the person's course veers, their life changes, they go to Africa and work with HIV babies; they move to Meir Sharim and throw stones at cars driving by on Shabbas. Ilan feebly answers himself that he could push the switch; really, he could. An even smaller voice whispers back: coward, asshole, pathetic. All of these people—this train—the bomb that should or should not go off, preposterous. Ilan imagines that his heart breaks a little for all these people who have the sad mischance to find themselves alongside him. Heartbreak, soul: what kind of words are these?

He moves again to take out Yedit's book, but Louis shouts in his ear, "Your god is an algorithm for wind, for snow, for coefficients of friction and probabilities of avalanches. You can't beseech him. He's a constant."

He's nothing more than a flashlight handle and a briefcase and a tingling burst of perspiration. He would like to take the book out of his chalice. Ilan would like to know what book the woman holds to her lap. *Behold your beauty, my delight, my desired, hinakh yafah*[22], *your eyes are pigeons from behind your veil, in the midst of your braids, your hair like a flock of goats, a herd of the strong (of refugees).* Perhaps the words of the song come to him because Hashem wills them so—but then why would God translate the *Shir haShirim* the way Yedit would? And if Hashem, may he exist, would indeed endorse a translation that makes his own existence impossible (or horrifying), then just maybe, that would be a Hashem worth worshipping. But where does that leave Ilan? What good is a god who refutes his own presence by denying his goodness? What good is a god? Ilan's heart rate accelerates rapidly in his stomach, unexpectedly, and he clings to the pole, gasps, struggles to steady himself. Again the *Shema* comes to his lips, quietly, furtively, the work of a secret inner self awed by a flash of the Shechinah in the sky. But he suppresses his lips' motion, suppresses the galaxy of *neshamot* that arranges itself before him, star coordinates traded in for SS serial numbers, turned to ash and scattered, sparkling across the winter night. It is bigger than his words, this flash, this comprehension. He can feel it like stubble above Anne's knee; but he can't speak it, can't know it. Only the *Shema* seems to know it.

"Because he's an algorithm," Louis whispers in his ear, "a constant, you silly Jew. Only a Jew would complicate being a hero. Only a Jew would feel guilt over the death of his enemy."

And Ilan thinks: Hashem gave the Jews the Torah so that we would not destroy the world. Yes, our strength is that we can feel shame at killing those who would kill us. Our strength, and, yes, clichéd as it is, our weakness. Steadier now, his pulse recedes to a throb in the tattoo.

Ilan squeezes the flashlight handle so that its pebbled pattern digs into his hands. He begins to rub his hand up and down it. This might scour the homeless woman's dead skin from his palm. Then he freezes. He might turn the flashlight on and light up the train if he isn't careful. Jerking his gaze from the woman's as yet unopened book, her breasts, her skin, he scans, scans, scans the car. Does anyone realize? Do they worry: is that a flashlight in his pocket? And he has to stifle a giggle.

He adjusts the handle so that it is vertically aligned and pulls his hand out of his pocket. And what if he was happy to see them? He should blow them up. This should be the train. Enough riding back and forth, day in, day out, with this stupid vest on. For once and for all, he'll put his hand back in his pocket, he'll depress the button: no more Herr Doktor Zizmor with his precious, smiling family.

Ilan opens and closes his left hand. Clammy. Contaminated.

They did rappel off the Pingora. The rope did not tangle. Ilan did not find himself mysteriously unable to control his descent, or suddenly plummeting as a bad anchor gave way. And as he lowered through the comforting vertigo of claustrophobically dense fog, an arc of image linked him to the moment in the stairwell of Tower Two after the dust from the impact settled and they'd begun walking down again, to the moment on the third day after he shot the Palestinian woman, when he found himself collecting the take-out containers in a trash bag, this moment on any of his climbs. They tell you that the climb isn't over until after you're back at home safe. They tell you that descending is the most dangerous part. It's all a ruse. It's to stave off that after-moment. A rainbow made of despair. The knowledge that you will make it: despair.

"Listen, Louis," Ilan contributes to the conversation he maintains with his nettlesome friend, even, especially, in his friend's absence. "The despair is in knowing that you can, in knowing, in the end, that life will return to normal, that all the poles and pulls that drove you towards this or that are still true. That at the end of the day, after the near-facing of rapture, you'll survive only to go back to Anne, to go back to the office, that your clients won't have left you, that you'll still be a sufficiently apt trader to make some real money from time to time. There's no triumph in succeeding.

"If we lived in an ecstatic world, after I shot that woman, I would no longer be able to be Ilan. If the world were ecstatic, the alpenglow of the fading storm would burst forth terrible chariots of destruction and all the plagues of Egypt would shatter us back into the earth from whence God summoned us."

Louis isn't on the train to answer all this. But Ilan imagines that if he were, he would smile and glow and hop from foot to foot to suppress the urge to interrupt Ilan with the answers he's already determined: 'survivor's guilt' and 'existential crisis' and 'post-deistic loss of meaning.' More infuriating still, Ilan can hear Louis' mock humility in his disclaimer that of course he suffers from those things too, we all do, who wouldn't. Ilan should realize that he's just like everybody else. We're all like everyone else. That's part of the despair, *bien sur*, for sure.

"But I'm wearing a bomb," Ilan mutters, contracting his abdomen and scowling, "I am wearing a bomb."

Hinach yafah rayahti. And the woman looks at him, her lips almost parting, her neck's arch stretching her posture. *Behold your beauty, my wife, my beloved; hinach yafah eynayikh yonim.*

Yes, Ilan thinks, doves. Eyes that from beyond the veil of her locks beak a sprig of an olive branch: land, land at last! *Behold the beauty of your eyes, doves.*

Is it this woman's eyes that at last mean shore? Do these doves tide an end of flood? Or do these eyes mean to fly, let-loose, gone, unreturning, unknowable.

At what moment did Noah find his despair? Was it when the ark floated? Did he realize he would make it then? Was it the discovery of Ham in nuptial embrace? Did that moment of violated sexual law bring relief to Noah, that second Adam made Adam by slaughter? Did Noah rejoice in knowing that man sprung from him would be as corrupt as the man from which he sprang? Was it the dove? Was it the rainbow? As soon as he could after setting foot on the ground, Noah made booze. The Torah relates it as if it happened instantly, but he had to grow the grapes, and the new vines take time before yielding fruit. Then he had to ferment it. Whatever the moment of that despair of knowing he would survive, it led to a dedicated plight of years (three years at least!) to get drunk. No, the rainbow was not Noah's friend. The dove was not Noah's friend. And when finally he drank himself into oblivion, his sons, as many sons of alcoholics must wish to do, castrated him.

Yes, Ilan acknowledges, Noah was a righteous man. But the woman's eyes, behold, lovely, are no sign of peace. At best, they assert a god who gives a land. And that land is no peace, but a chance to be crushed into the *adamah* from which you were summoned. *Shuvu b'nai adam.*

She inhales and her forearms tremble.

Ilan wants to see her book, to know what she reads that he might somehow know who she is. He fights the suspicion itching his left ribs that her sigh is simply for the time it takes a train to get from station A to station B, never quick enough, never on time enough. One does not relax on the subway. How can they, Ilan thinks, when they could be blown up at any moment? Just for going to work. He strives to look back up at Dr. Zizmor that he might experience again his disgust with the man, but Ilan cannot stop looking at the side of her neck. He wants to touch and he is afraid that he will touch. *Ben shaday yalin*[23]*: Between my breasts (my God) he will sleep, he will lie.*

She's Jewish, you know, he thinks. And he'd be shocked if she wasn't, looking at her. Yes, he answers himself, softly, dismissively, in the tone of one spectator to the voyeur over his shoulder, who doesn't quite realize the wildlife's skittishness, the wildlife's preternatural hearing, yes. But she's one of the Esthers.

And the voice over his shoulder can't resist adding: and they were created, at the beginning of time, along with time, for Persian kings. While God created man from desert dust, he molded her from a pale brown clay scooped from banks of Gan Eden's stream. *Yonim, doves.* Eyes are no landfall. Ilan lurches forward as the train brakes.

His hand almost pushes the button in his pocket out of dumb animal reaction to his loss of balance.

Clutch, he thinks. I almost clutched the button. And the sweat cools almost as quickly as it perspires. A quick rush and his body confines him again. They're stopped in the tunnel. They're coming, he thinks. Of course they're not coming, he assures himself. This happens two days out of three. Yet, amazingly, the passengers all look up, as if aware for the first time that they've committed themselves to a reduction of ore hewn from the hills (by dwarves! by troglodytes!) and hammered into a tube that hurtles through nineteenth century shafts beneath the streets, as if realizing for the first time that their seats are made from a substance derived from the long decayed matter of ancient animals too stupid to avoid tar pits, from rotting vegetation entombed beneath deserts. Sitting ducks, Ilan thinks and fights the urge to weep. Just a little weeping, he begs of himself. If he could just weep a little, for a few seconds, all would be well. But the train will not allow him that either.

The woman lifts one leg over the other, turning the book flat on her lap, hands clasped on top of it. What is the book? he wants to know. When will the train start moving? The first flush of sweat gone, his body feels remarkably ok. The cramp in his left calf that hobbled him earlier is gone, as is the gastro-intestinal issues that led him so far from the station. He inhales and straightens his spine. He might almost feel well enough to talk to the woman.

But, he reminds himself, once you start talking, you can't easily retract. What if she begins to talk, to explain something, and, worse still, she proves to be engaging, and then, mid-story, your GI issues return? How will you close your eyes and slowly breathe through your nose? You can't interject silent meditation into a conversation without attracting the wrong kind of attention.

Ilan stares at her book, at the hard brown edge of binding that protrudes past the pages and her hands. A tip of red ribbon separates a third of the text and he wonders whether it's a discrete bookmark or the bound-in cloth common to religious texts. He looks quickly up to her face and now her head's cocked to the right, the pointed top fold of her left ear exposed, hair pushed behind it, and her gaze on his briefcase. She can't possibly be one of those Christians who read the bible on the train to work. But then, he reminds himself, mightn't she be one of the orthodox women, one of the few living on the Upper East Side, who *daven shachris* on the train in the morning, murmuring the prayers to themselves while on the way to work? Could it be that this woman in front of him might be planning to recite the morning *Shema* down here on the train? Can Hashem hear and answer prayers from underground? Well that's a silly question, Ilan decides. If Hashem, then prayers from anywhere (but not necessarily heaven). And yet there are the long *mishnayot* on where prayers may be said. Not in a bathroom. Not in a place that's unclean. Not in place where there's a bad smell. He has to ask Louis if his conception of God allows for decisions or simply constants. Really, subways seem unsuited for prayer. But what if you were in a grave danger while in a place that was unclean? Could you pray then? And if you were confined to a Treblinka barrack, rotting typhoid dead hemming you, could you pray then? Would your prayer be rejected for lack of sanctified space from whence to issue it? And if he bends over now to take his own book of psalms, Yedit Manus' book of psalms, from his case, will he make eye contact with this woman? And will she look away or continue to look at him?

She turns the book over and he catches a glimpse of gilt lettering. English or Hebrew, he cannot tell. But gilt generally implies religious text in any language. He looks up from her book and sees that she's staring at him. This would be the moment to speak. Again words prove too heavy to easily gain momentum. He converts mumbled stuttering to a half smile and nods his head at her book. She turns up the tips of her lips and inclines her head, barely, to the left. Even the slight angle threatens to unleash her hair from behind her ear; it bulges there as the upper layers sluice over each other.

Her plaits, her veil, her braids, from beyond which, from within which, her eyes: yonim, pigeons.

Ilan runs his body through a series of checks to insure that he really feels ok. Surprisingly, his stomach doesn't bother him. He has no need to find a bathroom. He tries to build anxiety about the train's prolonged pause. Nothing doing. His attempts to hyperventilate in response to the beautiful woman sitting before him likewise fail. He cannot even get too bothered about the excessive warmth of the train car. No matter how he addresses the problem, all systems remain a go. Well then, Ilan thinks to himself, I guess I'm going to have to talk to her. And Anne? He offers up as a last caution. But even while doing so he knows that she is dismissible, or if not dismissible (clearly not dismissible: he's failed to rid himself of their relationship for six years now), then at least no hindrance to attempts to dismiss her through attempted amorous indiscretions.

Zeramtam: You washed them away. And yet still he stands. *You wash man from the universe because the flood's current is fast.* But he can speak. He has the capacity for speech. *Shenah yihiyu: They were asleep.* If Ilan opened his mouth it would be with charm and poise and wit. *They were inanimate, they were buried, they were dead to the things seen in sleep, in dreams.*

For once, Ilan feels, his dreams are not before him. The tattoo does not pulse. He is not plagued by the amalgam of snow, and Louis' rusting footlocker, and the sweat formed between his upper thigh and Anne's ass when they share, uncomfortably, a bed, and the Palestinian woman's eyes, and something else, something like a longing met with suffocating flames, that amalgam, that sleep-sight. *Like three hours of the night, Baboker kechatzir yachalof*[24]*: in the morning like grass sprouted (or vanished).* Or, as Manus muses: You washed them away: they will be asleep, in the morning they will be like grass, like weeds, grown only that in the next line we might learn that the new grass green at sunrise is withered by day's end, desiccated. Who are they? Who will be withered or washed, destroyed, by wet or by dry? The thousand years? The person who, in the lines above, You turned to dust in the echo of the instigation of earth and universe? A thousand years or people destroyed. Flushed in flood, they're like a sleep those thousand years, like a day, yesterday, elapsed, the thousand years it takes to build the known world and produce all of the people and all of the civilization, a thousand years, washed away in a flood (The Flood), like grass sprung in the night's cool, wilted by the sun's apex: three hours or four, a watch in the night, in their sleep or like a sleep. Whose sleep? Yours. You God.

Ilan gasps lightly and the woman looks up at him from her bent over posture, makes eye contact, his scalp tingles. She is the one.

The one what? The one girl? The one woman? Ilan's *basherta*? The other half of his *neshama* that Hashem separated from him before birth? The premises behind such a thing are ridiculous. And if God is a constant, an algorithm, the limited space of an infinitely small dimension, why couldn't there be a constant that defines the woman he must be with? Leaving aside entirely the deistically-fated aspects of the proposition, the statistically-encouraged sensibility that only one woman, or an extremely small number of women, might realistically complement, satisfy, heal, cure, complete, what-have-you, him, also proves absurd under examination. First of all, if Ilan accepts the premises underlying a statistically determined pool of suitable women—that a suitable woman must possess some specific group of characteristics that match or anti-match aspects of himself, and this in the absence of a benevolent (or even simply benign) god massaging fate into particular shapes—then he must also accept that there is no assurance that there is even a single woman who can be the, quote unquote, one. Furthermore, he knows nothing of this woman, can know nothing of her in the absence of time and speech. And perhaps, a voice, not Louis', but not dissimilar to Louis', suggests, that's why she can be the one, and she can only be the one for as long as you don't speak to her and don't know her.

Yonati behagve hasella, beseter hamadregah.[25]

Again with the *Song of Songs*? Ilan clears his throat into his fist and worries that he smells the slightest hint of homeless woman drifting up from his knuckles. The front of his scalp tingles with worry that his window of calm might be closing, that the train might never start moving again, or worse still, that it might. *My dove in the rock's crevices, in the step's hiding place;* or, *My despair cut into a coin, in hiding in the cliffs;* or, *Yonah, who climbed with my father, Dovid, up the rock's fissures to reach Yonah's father, Saul's, hiding place atop the cliffs. You who would betray for me, Yonah. Harini et-marayikh, hashmihi et-kolekh; ki kolekh arev, umarekh naveh.* Yedit Manus has become the pattern of his thoughts then, Yedit has taught him how to read. Unbidden, this song comes to him:

Because your voice is beautiful, because your voice is black, because your voice is sunset, because your voice will later assume the same adjective as my hair when my hair is compared to a raven. Let me hear your voice, let me see how you appear.

The woman flips her hair back further behind her ear and turns her head to look out the window. A line of muscle runs along her neck from her ear to the collar of her brown suit jacket and Ilan wonders how many Jews ever did get to live in that promised land of *tevel,* of milk and honey, of grapes the size of a man's hand. Of course, the people questioned God's deliverance, his ability to conquer those in the land; he'd ignored them for 300 years in Egypt, in slavery. And in response, to quell their suspicions, He let them die in the desert. Forty years of wandering. What people wouldn't question the god who left them enslaved for 300 years? Why should they believe He would now answer their desires? When their cries were no longer anguished? After he'd already allowed the murder of their sons?

Because God had finally, 300 years of slavery later, witnessed their tears, heard their cries, their pleas that He: remember Your covenants with Abraham, with Isaac, with Jacob! Because of that moment of action in which He used the opportunity to demonstrate with signs and wonders to the *eretz v'tevel* that He was The Almighty?

And was there ever a cry to God, unanguished?

Was there ever an anguished cry that didn't strive to remind God of his promises? Of his servants? Of his promises to them?

Why must God be so poor at keeping covenants?

Or is it simply that a thousand years pass in his eyes like a watch in the night, like a day that was yesterday and is over, like grass grown by morning, withered by night?

Why would God ever lapse in his covenants, whether for an hour or a thousand years?

Why would God cease to be God until his anguished chosen people's laments reminded him to be God?

Then every anguished cry to God is a demand that God be God again:

Hear, oh Lord, (remember) You are the Lord God, the one God of Israel!

He didn't answer you, Ilan, when you shot a woman to save your people.

He didn't answer you when you ceased to call his name.

He didn't answer you when you tattooed the outline of bullet on your chest.

In the void of God that God elided with creation, you have built a bomb, Ilan, and He has not answered you.

You have climbed a mountain to test your willingness to build a bomb, Ilan, and now you wear that bomb and He does not answer you.

But: *baruch sheim kavod l'olam va'ed.*

Even now, as the believers rise to power in Israel, the land seems doomed to loss again. Asshole, Ilan thinks, how can it not be lost if those who protect it tattoo the bullet wounds they inflict on their own flesh, shoulder the burden of those they rightfully kill? Who is God but the judge of death, killing's authorizer, its agentor, justifier, adjudicator?

And if God might authorize the shooting of the Palestinian woman, might he not also have authorized the bomb she bore?

The woman seated before Ilan makes a little noise, an impatient noise, and turns back forward. Did she think she'd be able to see through the window, down the tracks, see whatever it was that keeps them from moving? Her eyes turn up towards him again.

Let me see the way you are seen, let me hear your voice.

He wonders, what does she wonder? Her lips purse, her eyes still on his face. Horrified, he can feel his forehead wrinkling as his eyes pull ever wider, he cannot help but look back at her. He imagines a swallowing gesture coming from her, or a swallowing sound, he cannot tell which. Ilan swallows as well, nervous. To not speak now would be...his breath catches. And if she thinks: *to the mares yoked to Pharaoh's chariot, I have compared you, my delight.*

But that is Solomon's line; or if not Solomon, it's the male lover's. It could not be this woman's; she couldn't call Ilan her wife. She couldn't envy Pharaoh his mares; compare Ilan to Pharaoh's yoked beasts bound for drowning in the Red Sea. Or did Solomon covet Pharaoh's Pharaoh-hood? And if Jews triumphant lust for the symbols of their prior oppressors, could not this woman before Ilan speak the lines of a wooing king? Would he not deign to be her mare, her wife?

She could think that phrase. It is possible.

And to that phrase, Ilan imagines: *Al-taruni—Don't look at me—she'ani shecharhoret—for that I am blackened—Shehezaphtani hashemesh—that I am burnt by the sun.* Ilan gulps and the woman tilts her head, (*grass formed by morning, withered in the sun by day*). Speak! he pleads to her or himself, he cannot tell which. His legs anticipate, in small twitches, the grumbled movement of starting train wheels, but the train does not start, and her tilted countenance, *marekh naveh, yours which is seen is beautiful*, tells him: *kitapuach b'etze haya'ar, ken dodi ben habanim.* Ilan cocks his head opposite to how she's cocked hers and demands—not aloud, of course—how she can think of him as distinguished from the other sons as the apple tree is amidst the fruitless growth of the woods.

His vest bloats his figure. His eyes itch with last night's drink and a craving for the bottle *seter bahagve hasella*—no, not in its hiding place in the cliff, like Noah's dove, who had to flee first the waters and then the man who despaired at salvation, at land; not in hiding at all, but plainly atop the shelf set alongside his desk. Hundred-dollar single-malt Islay, because such a bottle is acceptable in his office. He uses it to spike his coffee. Irish Rose would serve just as well and save him eighty dollars twice a month; but, on his shelf, it would serve to get him fired.

He cannot tell whether it is the woman before him, or he, Ilan, who says next: *Samekuni, ba'ashishot-rafduni, ba'tapuchim: ki cholat-ahavah, ani*[26]. But he is certain that either of them would translate it the same way. Either of them would begin with *cholat-ahavah*, which cannot be translated as anything other than *lovesick*. And then, *Samekuni:* literally, *brace me*, or *support me, rest upon me*. Next, *ashishot: the pressed raisin cakes offered alongside sacrifices at the temple*, or really, anything pressed. *With ashishot rafduni: heal me.* And *ba'tapuchim: with apples.* Apples of the apple tree to which I have compared thee amongst the barren trees. *I am lovesick! Brace me, press me, heal me, with apples with raisin cakes, with your kisses, with sacrifice, by pressing against me, heal me, brace me, because I am sick with love.* Either of them, Ilan or this woman before him on the train would finish with: *because I am love-sick, because I am sick from love, because I am sick of love.*

And if the whole thing is really meant to be an allegory of Hashem's relationship with the Jewish people, then how lovesickness? How denial, and coyness, and apples, and distracting, yet meaningless, yet soothing, women?

Solomon taking solace in physical diversions, in the flesh of the many women already mares to his chariot; or, God too coy to be God: God pressed upon me, brace me, heal me; God turn me to crush me...

Dakka: crush; humiliate; humble; destroy: the verbs and nouns of each. In ashishot heal me.

Just lovesickness, Ilan urges himself to think (lovesickness for an absent God). He asks himself whether Anne isn't simply the safe base from which to pursue love. And the pursuit leaves him love sick, craving apples and upholstery, makes him nauseous with the illicit desire to call her, the destructive desire to renew whatever it is he had that he left for better.

"Kumi lakh, rayati, yafati. Ulekhi lakh."

And this, Ilan realizes, he has said aloud, though not loudly, but perhaps loudly enough to be heard over the incessant buzz of the stalled train, over the whine of the transformers that power the tubes that backlight The Zizomor family's salute and applaud.

The train lurches as if it was to the train that he had said, "Rise to me, my desire, my beauty. And come to me."

As if it was to the train he spoke, and the train had heard; and the train, amenable, lurches forward.

The tattoo inflates with his heart's pumping, swells. Ilan blushes. Heat flushes down his side. The woman's mouth opens slightly, closes, opens again. And then she speaks. She speaks softly and the train (jealous) is unbearably loud with the sound of crushing slate, the steel wheels on steel rails. He might have misheard her. She might have said to leave her alone, or asked him to repeat himself, his Hebrew unintelligible. But he doesn't think so. He's sure, and more sure because it surprises him, that instead she whispers with the cooing lilt of the harem's silk slip-doors parting:

"Ki-hine hasetav avar; Hageshem halaf, halakh lo."

"Yes," Ilan says, and he cannot tell whether his voice can be heard over the now moving train, the resumed reality, the incumbent world weighting over him as if he viewed the universe from beneath the floodwaters. *"Hanitzanim niru ba'aretz, et hatzamir higiyah."*

She smiles at him and shakes her head.

Ilan can hardly breathe. He hasn't read the *Song of Songs* since

Hebrew day school. How is it that the lines keep coming to him? How is that she knows them? He quickly looks behind him to see if either a) there's someone else she knows standing there; or b) whether Hashem is in fact hovering over his shoulder dictating his actions. He feels a moment of heartbreak for Anne, who he cannot possibly go back to now, not now that he knows that this woman, this Esther, this speaker of songs, exists.

This speaker of songs leans forward and holds her book up towards him.

"You've read my book."

He nods and smiles because that seems most appropriate, though he can't seem to synthesize the gilt letters into Hebrew words, can't tell if it's *that* book that she holds that he's read. Asshole, nodding and smiling aren't sufficient, say something more, respond. Ilan begins to open his mouth only to realize that he's trying to quote more of Solomon's song, only to realize that he's wearing a bomb. How passé, to be a bomber, now. How anticlimactic. He needs to form words, but nothing comes but random lines from the *Song of Songs* and a desperate warning to flee, *to brace, to press, to crush.*

If only he could hang on to the heart stone on his desk for a moment.

If only he could make the tattoo pulse loudly on his chest, loudly enough to drown out his thoughts.

If only the train would reach the next station, and the next, would let him off.

If only the train would stop between stations again, pause permanently, allow him to live out his life's remainder in gentle conversation with this niece of Mordecai, this twice-married Persian queen, this black-haired beautiful beauty; and he speaks, he says:

"It's been a long time since Hebrew School."

But she says, "*Echezu lanu shualim—shualim ketanim.*"

And he replies, "Saboteurs of the vineyards; and our vineyards blossom."

"Saboteurs?"

She smiles at him as if he's supposed to say something. But he has no idea how to trade pleasantries. If only she was the drycleaner, or the idiot woman from around the corner he ran into earlier, or a prospective client. If only, if only, if only, if only! What must Hashem be thinking to place two of his children on the subway train, one carrying a bomb, one carrying the *Megillot*'s pornography.

That's what's written on her book: *Megillot Miphorash*.

"You're reading *Shir haShirim*."

"Aren't you?" she asks.

But she's still smiling. Keep talking, he chides himself as the car rounds a robust curve, forcing him to clutch the pole. Ilan manages to not shake his head clear. In the process, he remembers an American Muslim quoted on the radio immediately after nine-eleven as saying, of Muhammad Atta, that to go face God with alcohol on one's breath was unthinkable. You have alcohol on your breath, he chastises himself. But do you believe in God? the Louis voice demands. Speak! Ilan orders himself and desperately manages to squeak out, "Is 'saboteurs' the wrong word?"

"Wrong word? It's not usual."

"Not usual; that means wrong."

Idiot! Asshole! What was that snickering laugh? You're a fucking grown man. You're a suicide bomber. Every Jewish woman in a fifty-mile radius wants to fuck you. Pull yourself together.

"I'd thought 'corrupters,' capture the defiling, but I rather like 'saboteurs' for the little foxes. *Mechablim* is a noun after all. Saboteurs of the grapevines. It's very Ben Gurion. The Haganah sneaking about the vineyards. Less illicit love, more sedition."

The back of Ilan's scalp itches and his right foot cramps across the arch. He needs to buy wider shoes. No, wait, what wider shoes. Who the hell is this woman? Why is he discussing the Haganah with her? Next they'll be talking about the IDF and was he ever in it, which leads inexorably back to the Palestinian woman. If only he was in some avalanche-ready cirque with Louis. At least he knows how to respond in those situations. At least he can have a drink when he climbs. You can't drink in the subway, not really, not in the morning, not while talking to some beautiful Esther in a perfectly polished suit who makes *mechablim* sound like a Zionist anthem.

"More Palmach than Haganah," Ilan manages, and immediately kicks the back of his shin as hard as he can. Idiot, asshole, idiot, what does that distinction even mean, idiot! "I like the defile connotation."

"The King James uses, 'that spoil,' but I don't care for that," she says. "Saboteur. Huh. Maybe. I'll have to give you credit."

This is your opportunity, asshole. She can't give you credit unless you tell her your name. If you tell her your name, she'll tell you her name. It has to work that way. But Ilan can't tell her his name. He's got a bomb strapped to his vest! He can't forget that. But so what? It's not like he's worried about getting caught; well not worried if he blows up, but he doesn't want to blow up. He can't ask a woman out knowing he might blow up! Come on: ask her for her phone number or something. Ask if she wants to go for a drink. Go for a drink? He'll repeat: he's wearing a fucking bomb! He can't in good conscience ask a woman to go have a glass of wine with him while he wears a hair-trigger explosive vest! It's indecent! It's outrageous! It just isn't right! Who would do such a thing? Besides, she's discussing Palmach and the nuances of Biblical translation. He'll look like an ass if he asks her for a drink. Hi, my name's Ilan, you seem real smart, wanna get drunk and be my girlfriend? Idiot. He can't do that. It'll just ruin things.

"You don't have to give me credit." Oh great, so now he's magnanimous. And Ilan's liver twists through his diaphragm because he does want to talk to this woman. He wants to touch her untouchable hair and carry her handbag and caress the book held between her lap and forearms. But if he doesn't get to his office, if he doesn't fill his coffee cup with ten bucks worth of the fancy Scotch, he'll start shaking and itching worse than Louis in an unclean bunker above the Siachen.

It's too late for Ilan.

His decisions have all been made for him. And yet there is always the hope that the bomb will not go off, that today is not the day, that today he will get to the office and take off the vest. (Maybe he can take a long walk at lunchtime; make his way past Peter Cooper Village and down to the East River; drop his vest into the tidal murk, another discarded life settling between sunken shopping carts and sunken eighteenth-century merchant boats. He'll want this woman's number if he does that, if he escapes the bomb after all.)

"Don't worry, my credit won't get you much anyway."

(The life that they will have together! He won't let her meet Louis until he is sure of their relationship. And, of course, there will be a night of tearful confession in his apartment, a necessary moment before he lifts his shirt and shows her the tattoo. When she sees it, she'll call him a clown and smack him on the side of the head, but lovingly, and hold him against her chest while he cries, finally cries, finally safe to do so. And then they'll clear the bottles out of his shelves, and he'll stop drinking, and she'll move in. One day he'll surprise her with a necklace of emerald beads bedded in a sandalwood box lined with myrrh. She'll tuck the scented twigs in her hair and languish down the hallway shedding clothes and tossing sprigs until there is nothing but her abdomen and her breasts, milk drops beneath a copper spigot, and the green gems across her clavicle and her heels on the end of the bed and her voice whispering, *bo alay, dodi. Ohavti lakh.* And he will say, "Yes, yes I am coming, my beloved. I am coming to you." And he will rise from her body as Bat Sheva rose from the *mikvah* into the blood-dusk of spring Jerusalem, the armies sent off to war. And this time he will not have to go to war. This time they will stay behind in a palace, a farmhouse they remake with their own hands, up the Hudson from whose upstairs patios they'll see the courtyards of the city down below. He'll have the kitchen he always wanted and she'll have a solarium as an office, the windows nearly choked with exotic succulents, her weathered teak desk bounded by living green. *A lily shoot yet of the Sharon; She'll be a lily of the valley.* Ilan might even one day tell her about this period in his life in which the absence-of-God yoked him to a bomb when he rode the train, when he met her.) Ilan realizes: he's wearing a bomb.

He's wearing a bomb and all he wants is to be held. He wants to be held by this woman in the farmhouse up the Hudson; he wants to weep, weep while this woman holds him, presses him. Ilan wants her to heal him, for he is lovesick.

There is no way that he can tell her he met her with a bomb around his chest, he knows that. There is no way that he can love this woman as he wants to love her, as an untouchable, (as a god), with that as a secret.

It is too late for him.

Asshole, he chides, and in chiding, reminds himself of how fatiguing this 'asshole' thing is anyway; asshole, he chides, say something flirty.

"What do you do?" he asks.

"That's not an interesting question."

No, it's not an interesting question. But then what is? He can't think of what else he's ever said to introduce himself to women. Then again, he doesn't particularly care for the women to which he's introduced himself. The vacuum in his chest begins to suck harder again, his Adam's apple threatens to fall down his throat. For some reason he mutters:

"*Pray, let us rise, raw, and circle the city, through the market stalls and the avenues, we'll seek that, our soul's love*: a morning bottle of wine."

"If we were to pace a perimeter, would the land enclosed belong to us," she asks, "as did the Promised Land to Avraham?"

"I'd settle for the bottle of wine," Ilan says. The pole has become slippery in his clutch. The vision of a cool dungeon of a bar, chairs still flipped-up on mosaic-tile-topped tables, seven or eight bands of light filtered through a louvered shade, makes anything possible. "Or, we could stay on the train until it reaches the Botanical Gardens."

"What a strange set of suggestions."

"We could do both," he says, "the wine and the gardens."

"Little saboteurs with wine amidst the vines?"

Ilan wants to say yes, but she is teasing him, clearly. He blushes, but nothing changes about her face. He's wearing this vest. She is opaque. He could squeeze her arm until it bruised and not know what he felt beneath the skin, tear at her face till her eyes swell shut and never know what she thinks. Who is she? He's afraid to move too quickly. Beneath whatever might happen to that stunning exterior, an unmarrable statue of this Esther will persevere.

He cannot afford to lose her.

And yet the Palestinian woman; and yet God. And yet that he would kill and love afterwards, and this woman, and what God? This, *that which his nephesh loves*, is a gift from Hashem. Jacob hid Dinah from Esau, and Hashem let a prince abduct her: perhaps, since Ilan is willing to give up everything: perhaps Hashem's gift is a woman who can save Ilan. Perhaps God only wants to see that Ilan would wear the bomb so that God could make it clear to the world that He never wants bombs again and this woman is the face of that forgiveness. Perhaps God is letting Ilan see the face of his delight, hear the sound of her voice, that Ilan might know that he need not mourn the Palestinian woman. Perhaps Ilan is saved.

And perhaps God has allowed all this that Ilan might know that God is God and that it is right that Ilan wear a bomb.

God, who lets Jacob hide Dinah, then punishes Jacob by letting a city rape her, then punishes the city by letting her brothers destroy it. No, Ilan thinks with debilitating hunger, with exhaustion in his thighs: Hashem doesn't fix; Hashem punishes. Then why was this woman sent to meet him? The question is so dark. Why must she be punished? Or there are no gods, not even Louis' little dimension.

To all this, Ilan barely says, "Why did I think to say, *winter was over, the rain vanished, walked further along*, when it's November, winter nigh upon us?"

"I can hardly hear you," she says, leaning in.

"But you understand."

"This is a subway. We're commuters. I'm no believer."

"I keep wanting to believe."

"What I want to know is why you translated *halaf* as 'vanished' rather than 'passed'?'"

"Why didn't I simply translate it as the *shochet's* knife?" he asks.

Ilan's heart rate accelerates again, but in a good way. I can handle this, he thinks. And everything around the woman's head blurs. His face warms further. Sweat forms along his sides and in the corners of his eyebrows.

She should reject his aggression, he thinks, but instead she says:

"So 'vanish' forces the reader to consider the word in a way that emphasizes the translation, 'slaughterer's knife,' without explicitly stating it."

He wants to pinch her lower lip while biting her upper lip. He wants to tie her hands to the handrail, pull up her shirt and flog her. He wants to put his head on her thigh and listen to her sing *Yerushalaim shel Zahav* while she soothes his hair. Yes, he understands why he might need Anne to bring him apples for he is sick with love of this woman.

"Who is this reader?" he asks.

"Who are my readers? Who knows: academics, maybe, maybe secular Jews who revel in imagining the zealots reading it. I don't know"

"I don't understand."

"Neither do I. I thought: my tenure committee will pretend to read it. My editor will read it, mostly, and then four other academics will look at it. If I'm lucky, some English department's 'Bible as Literature' class might assign it. If I get lucky. But I apparently have readers."

"For the *Shir haShirim*?"

"The *Song of Songs*? If I'm lucky, again, yes, with it too. I'll get the much wider audience. At least that's what my publisher hopes."

The stone house with hardwood floors and too much sunlight crumbles. *My lover sent his hand from the peephole.* Ilan cannot hold it together. Thistles sprout across the yard like marching beads of perspiration along an arm. Dandelions, weed-trees and willows mount an offence from the forest's edge. Deer wander up to the abandoned half-height walls, stray cats pounce through the empty windows and shit on the rotten flooring beneath a roofless sky. *I rose to open to my lover...myrrh fell from my hands...I opened to my lover, dodi hamak, my lover was gone.*

My soul, my self, evicted by his speech.

"You tell me," she says. "You're my reader. Who are you?"

"Who am I?"

"You've read my book, which makes you 'this reader.' Who are you?"

She can feel his vest. She can feel the bomb. Ilan is sure of it. Because how else can she be who she's becoming? (And is his bomb the psalm that finally reminds her that God is God? And is this woman on the subway the psalmist, this psalm's psalmist? And if he reminds her, does she not remind him, Ilan?) How can she be the peasant woman and Esther (and Manus)? She's even Sarah, in some way, the overly-beautiful jealous matriarch who bore her first child at a hundred years of age. This woman is turning out to be all of these. She's turning out to be the sister whose missives Ilan never heeded until she bore him with a book of psalms that have infected his brain and driven him to wear a suicide bomber's vest on a subway train. But she can't be.

She can't be Yedit Manus. What are the odds? How could it come to pass? No, such coincidences (Louis's constant's determined chaos) simply do not occur.

It's her bomb he wears, this woman's; her psalm he wears. He is her psalm.

"I should have explained. I'm..."

The train's halt deafens, thrusts her sideways into the woman beside her and Ilan's head moves with, follows, the pendulum sway of her breasts against her jacket's fabric. Here, he suspects, is an answer to a question posed on a mountaintop in refutation of a rainbow over storm clouds. No, he thinks, he never really wanted her to be the thick-legged peasant. His Adam's apple tingles and Ilan delicately—fearful of losing his balance despite the train's stasis, despite the already-late commuters' groans and mumbled curses—

reaches down to his chalice. She keeps speaking, excitedly, about her work: of her multiple translation technique, of the difference between oral and written, the complications raised by puns, the freedom of insight allowed when one stops thinking of the *Song of Songs* as an allegory for God's relationship to the Jewish people, and starts thinking of God's inaccessibility as an operative metaphor, a conceit really, for a lover's untouchable nature, for pain as beauty and worship.

"God is always the addressee," she says: God knocks on the door, and by the time the lover opens it, God is gone. God leaves her to wander the streets, her soul chasing his words. She wanders at night, lovesick, alone, and the guards beat her. And when the young man speaks, all he wants is for God to recognize that he loves Him anyway, despite the sun's effects or whatever, he finds God beautiful, just wants God to brace him, or press him down. He wants God to heal him.

"Couldn't it just be the other ways, that God's the metaphor for a lover?" he asks, hopes, though she speaks over him.

She says: the *Song of Songs*—song of which songs? Of the songs we call psalms, obviously—Song of David, Song of Moses, Song of the Sons of Korach, Song of the Chief Musician, Song of Solomon—aren't these all the same? They ask for the same thing: for the speaker to be reunited with the addressee.

And Ilan accepts: *Dakka,* in Psalm 90, as the penance of a man becomes *ashishot,* in Book 2, as the cure for the lovesick. To be pressed and braced; to be crushed. Both speakers pray to one absent because of the absence of that one, both plead prior commitments, both ask for healing in a crushing return.

Ilan struggles to ignore everything, and for a moment succeeds: December, a few days after his last birthday. He'd come straight home after work to get changed before going out. Louis' new girlfriend's best friend was supposed to go with them to dinner at Lupa and then to the Bubble Lounge. God, Ilan laments, is there anyone left in his life but Louis and Anne? Ilan's doorman stopped him as he came into the building to hand him a package. Seeing that it was from his sister and that it was clearly a book, Ilan set it on his kitchen table unopened. For years running, since he'd returned to the states, his sister had alternated sending him books on alcoholism and Zionist history, Hertzl and Ben-Itamar and Ben-Avi and Gurion, all of them. Ilan was back in the elevator heading down before he noticed the wine-stain on his shirt pocket, and had to head back up again to change shirts. By the time he reached Lupa, the three had sat down, which, since their party was incomplete, had cost Louis a forty-dollar-tip, or, rather, bribe.

Ilan half-bowed while apologizing and pulling out his chair. And then, chair half out, he assessed the woman Louis' girlfriend had brought with. She was stocky. Though that wasn't necessarily a problem. Her frizzy hair screamed: Long Island Jew. Though was he, a Pittsburgh Jew, anyone to judge? Her mascara was too thick and too purple so that her eyes looked like pulped concord grapes. Even that he could have been all right with. But she smelled slightly, as if she'd run for a train in her wool suit the morning after eating too much garlic. It was this smell, barely perceptible over that of ox-stew gravies and basil-based sauces, that was too much. Ilan knew that it was too much, and knew that it came from his prospective date, because he'd slept with her before. Then it's back to Anne, Ilan had thought, bracing himself for a night of not knowing if this woman who he hadn't called, hadn't called because he didn't like the way she smelled, would have what it took to ask him why he hadn't called.

That time was the last time: the package still lay unopened on a kitchen table that had never known the clutter of clipped wires and hastily mixed explosive, never known the detritus of butchered Donna Karan vests and butchered personal flotation devices. That time spent squirming in front of a woman he could not conceivably take home again (though he tried, out of manners, he claimed to Louis), and a best friend who thought the smelly woman was appropriate for him (insulting, even punitive, but deserved), that time was the last time that he hadn't yet known Manus's (Yedit's) psalms (when he was still but a lily shoot yet of the Sharon, its bud unbloomed). That time now strikes Ilan as idyllic, innocent, blessed. Because when he got home alone, drunk and still drinking, it seemed amusing to open the package so that he might skewer the book in an email to his sister.

He opened the package to reveal a cover that fancifully depicted King Dovid beheading King Saul. He opened the book's cover and found:

Happy is the man that hasn't walked in the counsel of evil-doers. Or so most translations would have you believe the first psalm in the ancient book of Psalms *begins. But what if we translate 'ba'atzat' to mean 'upon the advice of' rather than 'in the counsel of.' This makes more sense, of course. One more often follows advice than walks in counsel, but now the advice of our 'happy man' has become an incentive to go, to be active, to take initiative. This advice of these evil-doers is but a trigger for what the happy-man already possesses: his own evil inclination, what Chasidim would call his yetzer horah, his ability to innovate endlessly.*

The next line's syntax supports this reading. It begins, 'And in the path of sinners.' One walks down paths, the suggestion triggers a body of innovation, an inclination to walk down a path in which our Happy Man 'didn't stand.' But here we're back to a passive act untaken. Our hero has neither set off nor stood still. He is nowhere while sinners and evildoers abound. His happiness is tied to his absence. And so on and so forth, the text continued, seductively, enticingly, until one day Ilan found himself, like the 'happy man' who, Yedit—Yedit! She stands before Ilan—concluded, was only happy in death, in death where, finally, he could meditate upon God's Torah: meditate and never act.

Beset by evil-doers and sinners and buffoons, Ilan found himself staying in to assemble a vest.

He has beheld the face of his delight, his beloved.

She has let him hear her voice.

Her face, transcendent; her voice, harkening.

Eyesight blurred and bright, lips tense and pursed, heartbeat much too fast, head dizzy and light, Ilan stands with his book, with Yedit's psalms in his hands. He holds it up and she laughs, coy, pleased, lovable. Present finally. Touchable even. He could cradle her chin right now and he would feel her, would know her, could break through that barrier. Yes, an Esther corrupted. A ringing damnation of that God that refused and refused and refused.

"This is really you? For real?"

"Why do I feel like a rock star?"

She is so fucking charming. She is not hidden in a cleft in the rock. She is no dove. The waters will not recede. Ilan looks up to Dr. Z and Dr. Z looks back down at him. His stomach feels the way it used to before he did well on an exam. Louis was wrong after all.

Ilan knows why Hashem put her on the train, why He decreed this.

Ilan and his Esther, Ilan and Yedit. Asshole, Ilan marvels, he was created at creation! Created: Before God bore the mountains, formed the world and the universe. L'olam v'ad-olam, attah El! *Ilan puts his left hand in his pocket; looks at her, sees her.*

The train jolts forward a few feet, as if in answer, begins to roll again; the world begins to roll again and before Ilan loses it, he hollers at the top of his lungs:

"Shema! Yisraeil! Adonoi!"

Her eyes change: she knows; he knows she knows. But there is nothing else now. Now they are past even the lists of things abnegated by their listing: women and gods and travelers and psalms and future lives imagined and friends and mountains. Just her and him and the flashlight handle and The Lord, God. Yes: Hear! Israel! The Lord!

"Eloheinu! Adonoi! Echad!"

Endnotes

1 Psalm 20
2 Psalm 89
3 ibid
4 ibid
5 Song of Songs, Chapter 5
6 ibid
7 ibid
8 Song of Songs, Book 8
9 Psalm 124
10 Psalm 131
11 Song of Songs, Book 2
12 Psalm 19
13 Psalm 139
14 Psalm 90
15 Psalm 150
16 Psalm 90
17 Psalm 150
18 ibid
19 Psalm 90
20 Song of Songs, Book 1
21 Song of Songs, Book 2
22 Song of Songs, Book 4
23 Song of Songs, Book 1
24 Psalm 90
25 Song of Songs, Book 2
26 Song of Songs, Book

Acknowledgements

The making of a novel is never a solitary act, but in the case of *A Song of Ilan*, I am indebted even more than usual to encouragers, teachers, collaborators, friends, and believers. I am most recently and deeply indebted to Debra Di Blasi, publisher of Jaded Ibis Productions, who believed in this project after I had lost hope that it would arrive between covers. I would never have come to write *A Song of Ilan* were it not for Francois Camoin, who encouraged me to apply to the University of Utah, and in my very first workshop told me that a throwaway short story needed to be a novel, and then worked with me on this project for the following four years, insisting all the while that I make it more like Marguerite Duras' *The Lover*. Likewise, I am grateful to the University of Utah, especially its English Ph.D. program, where an earlier draft of this novel served as my dissertation. My classmates, teachers, and committee were indispensable to say the least, especially those professors who read drafts: Scott Black, Joseph Metz, Jacqueline Osherow, Matthew Potolsky, and Melanie Rae Thon; the friends who put up with infinite drafts: Matthew Batt, Rachel Marston, Christine Marshall, Alexandra Enders, Heather Laszlo, Emily Riehle, Cheyenne Roth Haven, Dean Winter, and Rich Wistisen; my many classmates over those years; and my favorite readers, Rachel Paul Motto, Aya & Dylan Keefe, Barbara Keiler, and Michal Woynarowski.

Portions of this novel have won the Utah Writers' Contest, sponsored by *Western Humanities Review* and judged by Alvin Greenberg, and the Richard Scowcroft Award, judged by Ron Carlson. The portion that won the Utah Writers' Contest was edited by Barry Weller and Pj Carlisle and published in *WHR*. I am also grateful for the current material and collegial support of my employer, High Point University, and of my colleagues in the English Department here.

Finally, I can't begin to express my great fortune in working with my collaborators on the art and music versions of this book, Van Goose (Shlomi Lavie) and Sarah Martin.

About the Author

Jacob Paul's 2010 debut novel, *Sarah/Sara*, was called one of that year's five best first fictions by *Poets & Writers*. His work has appeared in *Hunger Mountain, Western Humanities Review, Green Mountains Review, Massachusetts Review, Seneca Review, Mountain Gazette* and *USA Today's Weekend Magazine,* and on therumpus.net, fictionwritersreview.com and numerocinqmagazine.com. A former OppenheimerFunds product manager, he currently teaches creative writing at High Point University in North Carolina. More information may be found at www.jacobgpaul.com

About the Collection

A Song of Ilan is published in black-on-cream paperback, and full-color illustrated print and ebook, with original art by Sarah Martin. Music on the album, *Dark Rather Than Tan,* was composed and performed by Van Goose especially for *A Song of Ilan,* and is available at cdbaby.com, iTunes, Amazon, and other digital music download sites.

www.ingramcontent.com/pod-product-compliance
Lightning Source LLC
Chambersburg PA
CBHW020019030726
47499CB00007B/2179

* 9 7 8 1 9 3 7 5 4 3 8 8 4 *